Ten Days One Guernsey Summer

by

A V J Brassell

Dedication

This book is dedicated
to the loving memory
of my Nan and Grumps.

Their evacuation story was the
inspiration for this book.

They are pictured on the back cover in their home
shortly after the war ended.

Cover Photo

Heinkel 111 over Castle Cornet in St Peter Port

With thanks to my beautiful wife Christine for all her support.

First Printing, 2017

ISBN-13: 978-1548225391
ISBN-10: 1548225398

Foreword

Time is an amazing concept, our knowledge, our beliefs and our skills can be based on our family history. The remarkably impulsive and brave exploit of my Grandfather which was the inspiration for this book, offers a link to a past we can barely understand. When I heard this story, he was my grumps, born just after 1900 in the Cape of Good Hope, then a British Colony coloured pink on those old maps which had been drawn when the sun never set on the British Empire. He was born into a military family but had the good fortune to never fight in the first or second world wars, being too young for the first and then too old for the second.

When he told me his stories of Ireland and his war time experiences, I never took enough notice and now he is long gone. But I wonder if he was the same. Did he listen to tales of his grandfather and grandmother? Given average age profiles, those men and women may have had recollections of news of Gettysberg and the American Civil War, seen the young Queen Victoria or remembered the Boer War and other major events. They could have told him tales of their grandfathers and grandmothers and their experiences in the war against Napoleon, their memories of Trafalgar, Waterloo and the advent of steam engines and other wonders of the Industrial Revolution.

That man had the potential to give me a direct link to the past, but I was young, and history was a subject at school which ate precious time that I would rather spend playing football.

My reason for writing this book is to capture a moment in time, convey it as he might have seen it, and store it for future generations to read and understand. I also hope it is an enjoyable read and brings back memories for some, excites others and perhaps inspires a few others to listen to their grandparents and record the past before it is too late.

The exploits of my grandfather and grandmother are fact, they told me how they left the island and the terrible decisions they had to make, but for the purposes of this story, names, dates and even the sequences of events may have been adjusted to help the tale and to emphasise the immensity of the decisions that had to be made.

This story is based on the events that happened in the summer of 1940 in the beautiful, peaceful and sunny island of Guernsey, one of the British Channel Islands.

Introduction

Guernsey is a small island in the Bay of St Malo. One of the British Channel Islands, it is around 24 square miles in area and has a population of around 65,000. Historically it was part of the Duchy of Normandy in the time of William the Conqueror and Guernsey men may have accompanied him and his knights when they invaded England and defeated Harold at the Battle of Hastings.

As a reward for their success, landowners in Guernsey were granted great tracts of land in England and that ultimately resulted in the decision in 1204 for Guernsey to swear loyalty to King John and remain part of Great Britain, rather than swearing loyalty to the French King. A few hostages probably helped as well. Over the next 150 years or more the French made several efforts to capture the Channel Islands, and were occasionally successful, but the islanders were loyal to Great Britain and eventually stability was achieved and Guernsey and the other Channel Islands became loyal Crown Dependencies, part of Great Britain, but with the right to make their own laws and run their own lives.

That was until 1940.

Despite many scares during Napoleonic times and losing a large number of men during the first world war, island life had proved relatively stable and by and large economically successful. Ship building, trading, quarrying, tourism, horticulture, agriculture and fishing had been the way of life for the hard working "little people of Guernsey" as Victor Hugo described them. Then Europe, and later the world, became gripped in a second big war. By the time the second world war started, the Guernsey militia no longer existed, as it had in the first world war, but the young men of the island signed up, as they always had, to fight for King and Country. The British military presence on the island slipped away and the island was declared a demilitarized zone. France fell and

Britain stood alone. Guernsey and the Channel Islands stood in full view of occupied France, a tempting target, British to the core and ripe for picking. To some people living in Guernsey, it seemed inevitable that the Germans would come, but others hoped the islands would be left in peace. Decisions had to be made.

The summer of 1940 would change people forever and life would never be the same again for every Channel Islander.

This is the story of just one family caught up in this momentous period of history, little did they know how their lives would change, little did they know how decisions made then, would lead to new lives and new experiences. They had just a few hours to toss the coin of destiny and make the biggest decision of their lives.

What would you have done?

Prologue

The Bus Home

In a cloud of black smoke, the green and cream Dennis Falcon No 10 bus coughed into life. At walking pace, it pulled away from the throngs of people waiting to go home, leaving the tree lined Bus Terminus in St Peter Port, the capital of Guernsey. It was 5.30pm and the bus was mainly full of men heading home after a day's work. There were also several women with young children on the bus. Most of the mums were carrying bags full of shopping bought in town, as the main shopping area in St Peter Port was known locally.

At the next stop It pulled up in front of Laurence Dodsworth. He was waiting in front of the old water pump alongside the gardens behind the main offices of the States of Guernsey. The driver opened the door.

'Hop on Laurie,' the driver called out.

'Cheers Fred.' Laurence replied with a smile. 'Home James and don't spare the horses,' he added as he gave Fred a penny for his ticket. Fred laughed and revved the bus engine for Laurence's benefit. A couple of severe looking women in the front of the bus gave Laurence a disapproving frown as he walked up the aisle. He ignored them.

He was lucky enough to find the last window seat on the right-hand side of the bus and sat down just as the bus continued its journey north towards the Bridge, in St Sampsons, the island's second largest harbour. Laurence sat down and looked out towards the boats in St Peter Port Harbour. Between the cranes, he could see Castle Cornet which protected the harbour, and further out the islands of Herm, Jethou and Sark.

The woman next to him had been forced to move her bags so he could sit down and she looked decidedly unhappy about the "intrusion" into her space.

He watched as the harbour slipped past enabling him to enjoy the view across the Little Russell, the stretch of water between Guernsey and Herm. In the far distance, he could now make out a low grey streak on the horizon. It was the island of Jersey, the largest of the Channel Islands. He found himself squinting to see it properly. *I need new glasses*, he thought.

Laurence was a tall man compared to many on the bus, measuring 5 foot 10 inches in height. He was born while his family were on military service in South Africa, he was not local to the island and to many was considered an outsider. The average Guernsey man was 4 inches shorter than Laurence and the women shorter still. His wife, a Guernsey girl, was a full 12 inches shorter than her husband.

He wore a light brown tweed jacket with leather patches on the sleeves and dark trousers. He had a brown cap on his head and under his jacket he had a cream linen shirt and a brown patterned tie. He wore round, rimless glasses, a fashion of the times. He needed them to see anything further than a few feet in front of him. His cuff-links were Guernsey crests with the three leopards in gold on a red background. He had become a proud Guernseyman.

Laurence's shoes were light brown and highly polished - a remnant of his military days. Laurence polished his shoes every morning and he even kept a spare shoe cleaning kit in his desk at work, in case his shoes became dirty during the day. A tin of Cherry Blossom Boot Polish was never far away.

He was extremely organised, everything had to be neat and tidy. Nothing could be out of place.

His small moustache, which was starting to show a touch of grey, also hinted at a military bearing, as was his habit of nearly always standing at attention. His wife reckoned he even sat at attention.

Laurence gazed around the interior of the bus and noted the new green seat covers. He was just getting used to the new bus colours, as the Falcons had just been repainted from their old red and cream livery to the green and cream livery of the Guernsey Railway Company. *What a waste of money*, he thought.

'I am sure they have better things they could spend their money on,' he said to the woman next to him, pointing at the new seat covers.

'Well I like them,' she said, turning away to avoid further conversation.

He smiled to himself and went back to looking at the view rolling past.

The air was thick with cigarette and pipe smoke as nearly every man on the bus was smoking. Laurence had never tried a cigarette, he just didn't like the smell and it was a luxury he neither wanted or could afford. At 7p a packet that was the equivalent of a weeks' worth of bus journeys.

He also hated the way these bus journeys made his clothes smell of smoke and his wife often commented on it.

He sometimes avoided the bus just because of the smoke but today he wanted to get home to his family as quickly as possible. Every minute they spent together was precious and he hated it when they were apart.

People inside the bus were chattering away to each other and some were speaking in Guernsey French. He recognised a few words, which he had picked up from his wife, but English was his first language.

Laurence recognised a few people on the bus but wasn't in the mood to talk to anyone today. He liked to keep himself to himself most of the time and anyway he had a lot to think about.

Though you wouldn't think it, looking out of that bus window, all was not well in the world. The beauty of his island home, the wonderful view, the happy chatter on the bus and the wonderful life he led, all pointed to an idyll of epic proportions. At that time, the problems of the world seemed to be a million miles away but those problems were constantly demanding his attention. He needed time to think.

As he sat on the bus making its slow journey to his home, he unfolded and read the evening paper. The date on the top of the paper was Tuesday, 18th June 1940 and Germany had occupied most of Europe. The paper was full of stories of the war. Beyond, and to the north of Herm, Laurence could just make out the Cherbourg peninsular, some 30 or so miles away. He tried to imagine what was happening there and how the French must be feeling now they were occupied.

His wife came from a French family and they had distant relations living in the Cherbourg and Normandy area. He wondered how they were faring under the German jackboot and if they had survived the invasion of their towns and villages.

Looking over the top of his paper he could clearly see columns of smoke rising over where he believed the town of Cherbourg to be. He could only imagine the bitter fighting that must be taking place and the devastation the people must be experiencing.

A bit of him wished he was there, fighting against the old enemy, the Bosch, making a difference and saving people's lives. He had been ready to fight in the first world war and grew up playing at being a soldier, but the war ended before he could join his older friends and relatives on the Western front.

The death toll had been enormous but he would have gladly gone to join the British Army. He had believed in the cause and had hated the Germans for what they had done to Belgium and France.

The army was in his blood, as it was for many young people in the early years of the 20th century. War had been frequent and bloody and he knew this one was going the same way. Untold thousands had already died across the small strip of water he was looking at, and he knew thousands more would have to die before Hitler's German storm troopers were thrown out of France and the other occupied European countries.

As his bus journeyed towards the north of Guernsey, the last of the British Expeditionary Force was leaving Cherbourg, under fire from the advancing German army. Unlike the evacuation at Dunkirk, this withdrawal was more orderly and the troops left with most of their equipment. Once again all types of maritime transport had been secured to aid with the withdrawal.

In those areas of France already occupied, Adolf Hitler and Mussolini toured the territories they had conquered while German troops were already walking the streets of Paris, taking pictures, reading their Guide books and drinking in French restaurants and Cafes.

The leading stories in the paper and many of the conversations around him on the bus concerned the possibility that the Germans would come to the island. All the British troops had left and the islands had been officially demilitarized, but would the Germans leave the islanders to themselves, or would they seize the chance to take a little piece of British soil?

Focusing back on the newspaper, he noted that Delamares was having a boot sale and the children's plimsolls were just a shilling a pair. He thought that he might take Michael at the weekend to get a new pair, he was always wearing them out kicking his football and he was growing fast. Fuel was starting to be in short supply but the biggest advertisement on the page showed that Luxicabs were still offering a service. Telephone 666 was the headline, boasting that you could hire their cars for as little as 6 shillings an hour. That seemed a fortune to him.

As he read on he noted that there was a shilling fund for wounded Guernsey servicemen and he made a mental note to find out more and perhaps invest a few shillings.

Rationing had been introduced just a few months earlier and new ration books were being issued, which would come into use on July 8th. *Another job to do*, he thought, otherwise they would go short of meat, bacon, sugar and butter. He couldn't imagine a life without meat. More important for them was the announcement that primary schools were to go on holiday, with immediate effect, for a month. That might cause them some difficulties as Rachel was at Primary school and would be frustrated at not being able to go to her lessons and see her friends.

His mind and his gaze drifted again to Cherbourg and he wondered if the people there had thought the Germans would leave them alone, if they had hoped the advance would halt before their town fell to the enemy.

The more he thought about it, the more he believed the Germans would come to Guernsey. It just seemed inevitable, nothing seemed to stop their inexorable advance. The question was how they would come and whether it would be a peaceful visit, an attacking visit, or a full-blown occupation? He guessed only time would tell.

The one thing he had convinced himself was, that they had plenty of time. He was sure the Germans must have bigger things to think about than the tiny Channel Islands. After all what good were they to Hitler and his Nazi regime.

His attention drifted back to the newspaper and he was shocked to read that all dance halls and cinemas were to be closed. He wondered how, without that extra money, he would earn what they needed to feed the family. He had grown to depend on the extra income generated by his small band.

Laurence was their drummer, a skill he had acquired in the army, and they had a dance booking for that Saturday.

The paper also had a notice calling for volunteers to be Air Raid Wardens. He would sign up for that.

He put the paper down and stared out of the window again.

Laurence had come to the island purely by chance. Brought up in London, where some of his family still lived. He had worked on the railways for a while after his military service, then in 1930 he applied for a job with Southern Railways when they opened their new ferry service to Guernsey, using a ship called the 'Isle of Guernsey'. Jobs had been few and far between and when it was announced that they needed staff to work in Guernsey, he had jumped at the chance, preferring the prospect of a job in the sun to another summer in smoky old London.

It was in Guernsey he met his wife to be and instead of heading home after that summer season, he had stayed. That was nearly 10 years ago now and he was happy in the island. Life in London seemed a lifetime ago and he had never been back to the mainland.

Not known for being very sociable outside of his family circle, he refrained from joining in the conversations that were taking place all around him. But he took a lot in, listening to the many 'expert' opinions being put forward and smiling to himself when things were said that he knew were wrong. Sometimes people mistook his silence for ignorance but those that knew him also knew that when he spoke he was worth listening to.

He had spent the 18th June in the Southern Railway offices on the new jetty in St Peter Port Harbour processing papers, mainly to do with tomato exports, which were, up to this point unaffected by the war. Their ships also carried passengers and were in direct competition with the Great Western Railway ships which ran to Weymouth. All other crops had been stopped due to the threat to the islands and the only other major cargo the boats were carrying were people and the mail.

Many Guernsey residents had already decided to leave the island as the threat of invasion got closer. The smoke he saw over Cherbourg emphasised the nearness of war and many people with families in England and further afield were moving away to be with their relatives until the future for the Channel Islands became clearer.

He flicked to the Home service listings in the paper for the day and made a note that Stage Door was on at 9.35pm. They would tune in once they had finished supper and after the children had gone up the wooden hill to bed. It was also suggested in the paper that we should be digging for victory. He wished they had a garden as he knew his wife would love to grow their own food, but all they had was a back yard and a few tomato plants in pots, which she lovingly watered every day.

There had been more air raids on Malta according to the paper and that made him think of the potential for raids on Guernsey. At that point, he gave up the idea of reading anymore and folded up his copy of the paper and took in the scenery. The bus seemed to stop every couple of minutes as its cargo of passengers started to get off at their respective stops along 'the front', as the locals called the main road between St Peter Port and St Sampsons.

Herm, the closest Island to Guernsey, lay bathed in the summer sunshine and the White House Hotel stood out against the green hillside. A bonfire burnt on the island, sending a small plume of white smoke into the air to drift on the gentle summer breeze. The island of Jethou lay next to Herm, it's green slopes seemed to glow in the late afternoon sunshine and further in the distance the island of Sark could be seen clearly.

A few buildings could be made out on top of the Sark cliffs by the glint of the sunshine on their windows.

As his eyes took in the amazing view, two dark shapes appeared in the sky from the north. Heading towards Guernsey, they soon materialised into aircraft and Laurence could out the black crosses on the fuselage.
Conversation on the bus stopped, as did the bus, as all eyes including the drivers were trained on the aircraft as they headed low across the sea towards the island. Banking to the south they flew parallel to the islands east coast and came close enough so that all on the bus could make out the pilots and co-pilots of both aircraft.

'They're watching us.' Laurence announced to no-one in particular. He was convinced they were deliberately observing Guernsey, reconnoitering the island, checking for any defences.

The truth was far different, the two Heinkel 111 bombers were part of Kampfgeschwader 55, an attack group that were an advance unit of the Luftwaffe. They had just taken possession of the French air force base at Villacoublay, just south-west of Paris. The two planes had been dispatched on a mission to support the battle for Cherbourg and harass coastal shipping.

After their bombing runs the pilots had been drawn to the islands, fascinated by the sight of these little pieces of British soil. Having flown around Alderney and then on to Guernsey, they watched a green bus pull up near some tram sheds on the coast road. The lead plane waggled its wings and the sharp eyed on the bus could see the pilot wave his hand at the watchers. The planes banked over St Peter Port harbour and then flew east towards Sark, passing Jersey's north coast as they headed back to France.

The driver started the Dennis Falcon again, with its customary bang and cloud of exhaust smoke, and they drove on. Conversation on the bus started up in earnest, all were talking of their encounter with the German planes. Laurence simply stared out of the window, in a world of his own, and shortly after, got up from his seat to get off at the halfway, a point directly between the two towns, and where his little terraced house was situated.

He couldn't wait to tell his wife and children about the German planes.

Returning Home

Feldwebel Bernhard Schmitt knew Guernsey from the 1930's. He had visited the island whilst on holiday in England, taking the train to Southampton on the south coast and then catching a ferry to the island. He was a young man then, just 18, a quiet, studious boy, working on a history project based on European Wars. He was studying William the Conqueror and the invasion of England in 1066. The reason for the visit was to assess how the Channel Islands may have played a role in that invasion.

While in Guernsey, Bernhard had visited Castle Cornet and the island's Priaulx Library where he had read local historical papers. He had even visited the island's Greffe, where Guernsey based companies were registered, and many historically important documents were kept. There, he had seen the original Charters granted by various Kings and Queens of England, giving the island the right to make its own laws.

He had been in the island for just under a week and then travelled across to northern France before returning to England. He had promised himself that he would visit again to see more of the island and perhaps stay longer. He never imagined he would see Guernsey again in these circumstances.

In 1937, after completing his education in Germany, he had been swept along with the martial enthusiasm for the Third Reich and signed up with the Luftwaffe for pilot training. By the time war was declared he had received his pilot's wings and had been designated for bomber training. The training had been fast and furious and in the few months after qualifying, he had given support to the attacks on Poland, flying many successful missions.

As the Battle for France began he gave aerial support to ground troops as they pushed forward in what had become known as the tactic of *Blitzkrieg*, until in a matter of a few weeks they had reached the channel coast at Cherbourg. Except for a few easily repaired bullet holes, he and his crew had been unscathed and he was considered a lucky pilot.

Now, he and a few of his colleagues from Kampfgeschwader 55, were billeted in tents near Paris at Villacoublay and using that occupied airport to support the battles for Rennes and Cherbourg. He had also been ordered to make the occasional raid on coastal shipping, when required.

Villacoublay was also being used by Jagdgeschwader 26, a front-line squadron of Messerschmitt Bf 109E's. He had always admired the fighter boys and their swashbuckling way of living. They seemed to always drive fast cars, be followed around by gorgeous women and be wearing the best uniforms. The cult of the Red Baron from the First World War was still alive and well. He had noticed that many of the fighters lined up alongside the runway had battle honours and personal insignia as their pilots strive for glory and the legendary 'Ace' status. *Maybe I'll apply for fighter training one day*, he mused, but the truth was he loved his crew and he loved flying the Heinkel 111.

On the 18th June, he had been ordered to carry out a raid on Cherbourg and afterwards search for allied coastal shipping in the Bay of St Malo. Bernhard's crew was made up of his Radio Operator/Navigator and long term friend Unteroffizier Wilhelm "Willie" Schroder and two gunners, Kai, who was also the planes mechanic, and Karl, better known as the two K's.

Together with their wing man Feldwebel Schulz Barhoff and his crew, they had dropped their bombs on military targets on the outskirts of Cherbourg and then headed towards the Channel Islands to look for naval activity. The two K's were eager for a target and to test their prowess. They were always arguing about who was the best shot.

They had been through a lot together and they were more like family than crew.

The Battle for Poland had been an easy introduction to the war with Kampfgeschwader 55 suffering the loss of just one crew. But once they had moved into French airspace things had become more difficult, and many of their friends were already missing presumed dead in the Battle for France.

As French resistance eased and the British returned to their own soil, the battle had calmed down and for the first time in many weeks Bernhard felt at ease with their progress and looked forward to a better future. As far as he was concerned the battle was virtually over, he believed that Hitler could negotiate a peace agreement with their old allies, the British, and once that was done that would be the end of the war. He couldn't wait to get back to Germany and lead a normal life again.

Seeing the islands spread out before them had brought back many memories. They first flew over Alderney, noting the mile-long breakwater that had once protected the British fleet. When they reached Guernsey, Bernhard spotted the impressive roof line of Elizabeth College and the Victoria Tower which sat on the hill above St Peter Port. He even thought he could make out the Priaulx Library amongst the trees above Candie Gardens.

As they travelled along the island's east coast he had spotted an old Green Bus on the coastal road grinding to a halt, and he could make out many of the faces staring up at them. A little girl waved and he smiled and waved back, waggling his wings as she and the bus disappeared out of view.

Banking left over the busy harbour of St Peter Port they headed east towards Sark, before heading back towards battle torn France, passing along the cliffs which made up the north coast of Jersey on the way. As they flew, Bernhard pondered the future of the islands and whether the Army would invade. He saw little value in these small dots in the sea and they were obviously undefended, not a shot had been fired.

Perhaps we'll leave these people alone, he thought. He couldn't contemplate such a lovely place being attacked and suffering the same hardships he had witnessed in Poland and France.

After crossing the French coast, he circled around Paris to line up on the runway into the prevailing westerly wind. Throttling back, he eased his Heinkel 111 down on to the airstrip at Villacoublay, with hardly a bump. Another successful landing after a faultless mission, which was loudly applauded by Willie and the two K's.

After taxiing close to the control tower, he powered down the engines, letting them idle as he switched off the fuel. Once the props had stopped turning they abandoned the plane to the maintenance crew and he led the way to the de-briefing room. There he told the Oberleutnant what he had seen.

As usual his crew were happy with their work and they would soon be toasting another successful mission with a Schnapps or two. They left the de-briefing laughing and joking about who should buy the first round.

Oberleutenant Holstein had listened with interest and made detailed notes. After the young pilots and their crew had left, he picked up the telephone and reported back to the Kampfgeschwader 55's home base in Schwabisch-Hall.

From there the news that the islands were undefended was fed back to the Führer's HQ in the Felsennest, near what had been, the German border with Belgium.

Adolf Hitler read the report himself and smiled.

Anything to do with Britain was given express clearance to his desk. Orders were given and plans made.

Supper Time in Guernsey

Laurence Dodsworth got off the bus at the halfway along with three other passengers and he walked the short distance to his house. Laurence's house was a terraced property with views out towards the sea and St Peter Port from the upper floor. It had no front garden of any note and a small cobbled yard at the back. In the yard was an outside toilet and a large shed, with a corrugated roof, housing a large copper basin where his wife washed their clothes. It was also used for cooking crabs. Their neighbour owned a fishing boat and would bring them crabs when they were in season and if they were lucky, the occasional lobster.

There was also a mangle in the shed for drying the washing and space for a small workbench, complete with vice. The wall above the work bench provided space for all of Laurence's tools. He liked to work with wood in his spare time and was always tinkering with or repairing something. Everything had its place and many of the tools hung on the walls in their allotted spaces, duly labeled, so he always knew where they were.

Lilian, or Lily as she was affectionately known by all except her mother, was waiting for him. At 4 foot 10 inches she was a typical Guernsey girl. She was constantly busy, after all there was always something to do, especially with three children and a husband to look after. She flung her arms around his neck as soon as he walked through the front door and stretched herself up on tip toes to kiss him full on the lips.

'I love you my darling,' she whispered, with that lovely smile on her face. It had been that smile that had attracted him to her on the first day they met. He always said that her smile could light up any room.

'I love you too my love.'

Before he could say anything more a shout came from the kitchen.

'Daddy's home!'

The cry came from Rachel, their nine-year-old, eldest daughter.

A young girl with a shock of jet black hair exploded into the front hall and jumped into her father's arms. She still had her apron on, just like her mother, as she had been helping Lily prepare supper. Rachel was rapidly followed by Laura, who in contrast had long blonde hair, made even lighter by the summer sun. At five years old, she hadn't started school yet while Rachel was halfway through her time at Primary School.

'Dadda, Dadda, Dadda!' announced the arrival of Michael, Laura's twin brother and youngest child, by over a minute as Laura loved to remind him. Michael was a real handful, always on the go and wanting to be involved in everything that was going on, as long as it involved running. He had been in the back yard kicking a ball against the wall, dreaming of scoring the winning goal in the Muratti, the annual match between Guernsey and Jersey.

'Come and play,' he pleaded of his father. 'Come and play.'

Laurence politely declined, as he wanted some time with Lily after being at work all day. Michael ran off in tears, quickly followed by Laura who would, within minutes, be a reluctant goal-keeper as Michael tried to kick his battered leather football through the shed door.

'Be careful of my tomatoes,' Lily shouted after them as they went outside.

Rachel returned to the kitchen where she had been peeling potatoes. Laurence hung his jacket and cap on the coat rack in the hall and took Lilian into the front parlour and closed the door.

They sat down on the new sofa, it was Lily's latest possession and her pride and joy. Lacework covered the ends of the arms of the sofa as well as the back, to protect it from wear and tear, and Laurence's always Brylcreemed hair.

It was June so the fire wasn't lit but the grate was laid and ready to go, just in case they had a cold night. A small clock ticked loudly on top of the mantelpiece and in the corner, a larger grandfather clock ticked in time. A small radiogram stood on a table in front of the window and next to that was a large jardinière, with a healthy-looking aspidistra, adding a splash of green against the otherwise brown and cream décor of their favourite room. Several family photos added a personal touch to the immaculately clean room. Nothing looked out of place.

'I saw two German planes on the way home Lily, I think they might invade one day.' Laurence suddenly announced, as he began to relax into the sofa.

He passed her the Evening Star newspaper which he had purchased for a penny before catching the bus and she scanned the headlines. Lily wasn't one for reading much. She had grown up working in service from the age of 12 and had precious little opportunity to learn. What she did know, she had taught herself, but she understood clearly from the paper and from her conversations with her husband that tough times were ahead.

France was awaiting terms for an armistice but the fighting went on and she noted that the new ration books were being posted out. She was always worrying about how she was going to feed her family.

Lily had been shopping on the Bridge with Laura and Michael that day, and in the butchers the war was the only topic of conversation. On the way home, she too had seen the smoke over Cherbourg.

Lily looked worried.

'What would we do if the Germans came here?' She asked him.

Laurence held his wife close.

'Whatever happens my darling, we'll face the future together. Since we were married we've never spent a night apart, except for when the children were born, and I won't let someone like Adolf Hitler come between us now!'

They laughed, but it was a nervous laugh, full of doubt and confusion.

They hugged for a while until Rachel called out that the potatoes were ready. Lily gave Laurence a kiss on the cheek and mouthed, 'Must go,' before walking through to the kitchen, smiling as she always did when she was with Rachel. The two were so close, almost inseparable.

Laurence sat down, opened the paper and stared at the pages for a while, not really taking anything in.

He was startled out of his reverie when Lily called him through for supper. He gathered Laura and Michael in from the yard and sat them down at the kitchen table.

Lily placed plates full of sausages and mashed potato with fresh carrots and cabbage in front of everyone and then sat down with her family to enjoy their evening meal. Over tea they talked about the schools closing and what Rachel would do with her time off. The war would not be mentioned again that night until Laurence and Lily were alone in bed.

The children went up to bed at 8.30 pm and Lily spent time with each of them before coming back down to cuddle up next to Laurence. After playing a few records, quietly, not to disturb the children, at 9.35 on the dot, Laurence tuned into Stage Door. He and Lily enjoyed the voices of Dave and Joe O'Gorman and the entertainment they provided until it was their bed time. For that half an hour they could forget all the troubles they were facing.

After the show was over, Laurence remembered the news about the Dance Halls being closed and told his wife he wouldn't be playing in the band on Saturday. They agreed they would have to think about how to supplement his income but secretly she was pleased. Being left on her own every Saturday night was always a chore for her and she hated it.

I'll have to make him something special for supper that night, she thought.

Once they were in their bedroom getting ready for bed the subject of the war was raised again.

Their bedroom was a small room in the eaves of the house. They had a dark wooden dressing table, with matching wardrobe and a small double bed. A stand in the corner had a potted fern placed on top providing a splash of green in what was a mainly plain room. That was apart from the bed cover which was a knitted patchwork quilt of many assorted colours.

The walls were cream with white skirting boards with a matching white painted wooden slatted ceiling. This was Lily's second favourite room in the house.

'Do you think we should leave the Island Laurie?' Lily asked after she blew out the candle on the dressing table and climbed into bed.

She snuggled in next to Laurence who turned over and slipped his arm under her head so she could snuggle in closer.

'I don't know,' he answered honestly. 'I can't decide what is for the best.'

'The Germans are close now and it seems logical that they would come here eventually, but I don't think it will be for a while.'

'How long do you think the war will go on for?' Lily asked.

'I can't imagine the war can go on for much longer,' he replied. 'Six months perhaps. I reckon it will be all over by Christmas.'

'That's not long is it Laurie,' Lily stated. 'It would be nice to be all settled for Christmas.'

'One way or the other.' Laurence said quietly.

'What do you mean,' she asked.

'Well, it depends on whether we win or lose,' he explained. 'If the Germans invade England and win the war, we could be having a German Christmas. If the British hold them back and they agree a peace, we could be safe.'

Lily went quiet.

'Don't worry Love,' he reassured her. 'The Germans won't be thinking about us right now. If I were them, I would be planning an invasion of England, not Guernsey.'

'Are you sure Laurie?' Lily asked quietly.

'Yes dear,' he replied. Now let's get some sleep. 'I have a really busy day ahead.'

They kissed, and feeling safe wrapped in his arms, Lily fell asleep but Laurence struggled to get to sleep for quite a while.

His mind was full of thoughts about what the days ahead had in store and he had a bad feeling that this lovely life they were leading was going to change, and not for the better. Somehow his words of comfort to his wife seemed a bit hollow, the more he thought about the situation they were in and the events of the journey home, the more he began to believe that Hitler could well become a key factor in their lives.

As he lay awake he realised that if they stayed here and the Germans came, they might not like having ex-military men like him around. He could be considered a threat and taken as a prisoner to Germany. The Dictator could do what he always thought would be impossible.

He could split them apart.

Chapter 1 – Wednesday 19th June 1940

In the News

In France, the 7th Armoured Division under the direct command of Erwin Rommel heads towards Cherbourg. Hermann Goering orders the confiscation of all Dutch transport.
Horse Racing stops in the UK.
Germans Capture Lorient and Brest.

Guernsey

The day dawned bright and sunny and as usual the family were up bright and early. Lily had been down on the beach searching for driftwood to heat the copper, so she could wash some clothes and Laurence had helped make breakfast for all the children. Today breakfast was boiled eggs and soldiers, the girl's favourite start to the day. Michael pulled a face but ate his egg and soldiers anyway, leaving most of the white of the egg behind.

By 7.30am everyone was washed and ready to face the day. At 7.45 Laurence caught the bus to work. No seats were available today so he had to stand in the aisle all the way to town.

At 8.15 Lily set off with Rachel, Laura and Michael to spend some time with Lily's mum, affectionately known as Ma. She was always up nice and early too and loved to look after the children as it 'kept her young'.

She normally looked after Michael and Laura while Rachel was at school, but with the shock announcement yesterday that the schools were closed, Lily hoped she wouldn't mind looking after all of the children. Ma had a huge back garden and the kids would spend hours playing out there, climbing trees, feeding the chickens or digging for worms. Ma spoilt them whenever she could and her cream cakes were legendary. Later in the day they would all meet up after Lily had done her housework and they would go to the Bridge, to visit the shops and buy some groceries.

As Laurence's bus made its slow journey along the front, it passed rows of lorries. All were full to the brim with chip baskets, each basket full of almost ripe tomatoes. As the summer progressed, more and more lorries would join the queue for the boat.

Laurence got off the bus at the bottom of St Julian's Avenue, right opposite the Royal Hotel, and walked up the quay, passing more trucks full of tomatoes. As he was fascinated with trucks and cars, but had never learned to drive, he took more than a passing interest in the range of vehicles on display. Many were new green trucks that one of the larger local growers had just bought. The drivers stood around in groups smoking and chatting, resplendent in their matching brown overalls. Many said hello as he walked past, as they knew Laurence from the office. He was on first name terms with more than a dozen drivers and some lived close to where he lived.

He stopped and had a chat with a few of the drivers and one allowed him to sit in the cab of one of the new Ford trucks. He couldn't believe how high off the ground he was and what a splendid view he had from the driver's seat.

Some days, when he had more time, he would stop and chat to the drivers for a bit longer and talk about their work. He had dreamed of being a truck driver and travelling the world, delivering parcels to exotic places, odd in truth for someone who had never driven anything bigger than a bike.

Many of the vehicles were lovingly maintained and the classic names were on show, Ford, Morris, Bedford, with some models up to ten years old. Some of the newer vehicles were gleaming as if straight out of the showroom, as indeed they were.

Laurence tore himself away from looking at the trucks and hurriedly walked to his office on the New Jetty. As he was a clerk in the local shipping office of the Southern Railway Company he was responsible for the freight and passenger manifests for all their boats. From where he sat he could see the boats loading and unloading. It would be a busy day, typical of that time of year.

Cranes were busy lifting large nets full of tomato chip baskets on to the decks and into the holds of the boats moored alongside the jetty. Some crew members were carrying sacks of post and other miscellaneous freight on to the boats up narrow gangways. It looked chaotic but Laurence loved his 'view'.

Many times, over tea, he would regale his family with stories he put together from things he had seen from his view of the harbour. It amazed him that the men could walk along some of the narrow planks which connected the boats to the quay, he was yet to see one fall but was sure it must have happened more than once.

As always, the kettle was on and the phones were ringing. It was business as usual and Laurence was happy being busy.

The view from the window was soon forgotten as he got his head down and worked through the ever-increasing pile of manifests. The boats couldn't sail until the lists he was working on were complete, as the manifests provided the details of what cargo each ship was carrying.

Back in St Sampsons, Lily was soon walking around the Bridge with her mother and her children. Coal lorries regularly passed them by, delivering fuel to the greenhouses where the tomatoes were grown.

The harbour and its surrounds were a hive of activity, small boats came and went, while larger coasters unloaded coal on the north side of the harbour. A small oil tanker was tied up on the southern side of the harbour and a couple of fishing boats headed out to sea, following the tide.

A couple of people were hanging around with buckets and would scoop up any coal that fell from the lorries as they made their way from the harbour. Not everyone enjoyed the good life that Lily knew she had. *How lucky are we*, she thought?

Seagulls wheeled overhead and several headed out towards the fishing boats in search of fish scraps. Lily and Ma sat on a bench looking out to sea, while the children ate cream filled chocolate eclairs. One hopeful seagull stood and stared at them hoping for some crumbs.

Lily and her Mum could speak for ages, there always seemed to be something to talk about. Usually they spent their time people watching and in an island where everyone seemed to know everyone else, there was always gossip to share. They would also talk about people's clothes as they watched them walk by, admiring a nice coat or commenting on the particular colour of a dress someone was wearing.

Today it was all about the young woman in the cake shop and how apparently one young fisherman seemed to visit the shop every day to buy a cake.

'I think young Dan must be in love with that girl in the cake shop.' Ma stated in her strong Guernsey accent.

'Maybe he just likes cakes.' Lily replied laughing.

'Hope he washes his hands,' Ma replied. 'The smell of mackerel on an éclair would put me right off.'

After all, in a matter of a few months, the Germans had conquered most of Europe. She needed to talk to Laurence urgently but could she disturb him at work? She hardly ever went to town and had never been to his office.

An ambulance and the police were soon on the scene and the injured were being treated. The police took over the often-heated discussions with the desperate French evacuees,

After several minutes of deep thought and consideration Lily decided on action. Rather than waiting all day for Laurence to come home she would go and see him.

As soon as Ma came back Lily told her that she needed to talk to Laurence and asked her to take the children home. They had been looking over the railings at the refugees from France and she could see Laura and Michael were getting more than a little upset. She walked around the harbour to the bus stop and within ten minutes she was on her way to town. Within half an hour she nervously entered Laurence's office and waved the paper at him across the room. He got up and went straight over to her.

Laurence knew how difficult it must have been for her to summon the courage to come to his office. Something must be very wrong. Seeing Laurence's wife looking so upset the secretary put the kettle on and produced a cup of tea for Lilian as she sat in Laurence's seat. She looked so small and vulnerable behind the desk, her feet didn't even reach the floor and her eyes were full of tears. Laurence couldn't love her any more than he did right now. He walked behind her and kissed the top of her head and gently rubbed her shoulders to help calm her down.

'What are we to do Laurence?' she wept, looking up at him, the front page of the paper shouted that awful word at him from his desk. He gave the story a quick scan.

'We'll try and keep calm Lily for a start,' he gently scolded her. 'Please don't cry, it will not help and we need to decide very carefully what we will do next.'

'But Rachel, what will we do about Rachel?'

Laurence put his arms around his still weeping wife. 'We'll get out of here for a bit that's the first thing we'll do.'

He had a quick word with his secretary and then he took Lily out of the office and led her, hand in hand, through the mass of trucks to the Favourite Cafe, at the end of the Pollet, where he ordered two teas.

Lily had recovered some of her usual poise by the time they sat down. Laurence knew he had to be back in the office soon as he couldn't afford to lose his job. He felt like he was playing truant.

The Favourite Café looked out towards the weighbridge at the end of the quay and they sat at a small table by the window, though today the view was ignored.

'What shall we do Laurie?' Lily pleaded of her husband, nursing her cup of tea in both hands as if she was keeping her hands warm.

'We'll need to decide what is best for Rachel.' Laurence replied. 'She is so precious to both of us we need to know that she is safe.'

Lily nodded, staring at her cup. She just couldn't imagine not having Rachel around and was fighting hard not to cry again.

'Look my Love.' Laurence continued after a brief pause. 'I need to get back to work and we need to talk about this properly.'

'I'll try and get home early and then we'll go somewhere quieter than this and talk about the options.'

Lily nodded again. He wanted her to say something.

'What are you thinking Lily?' Laurence asked his wife, reaching across to hold her hand.

'I just can't bear the thought of losing Rachel, Laurie,' she whispered. 'I just can't bear it.'

Laurence got up from his chair and went around the table and bent down to put his arm around Lily's shoulder.

'I know my Love,' he whispered into her ear, kissing her head at the same time.

'Let's finish our tea and talk about this properly at home.'

He kissed her again and went back to his seat.

They both knew that whatever they decided, they would need to act quickly as they would need to register Rachel that evening for the evacuation which was scheduled for first thing tomorrow morning - if it was agreed she should go!

They finished their cups of tea and Laurence gave Lily a huge hug before sending her off to catch the bus home. Although Laurence had given her some pennies for the bus, she felt she needed time to think, so she walked back home along the beautiful sea front.

It was hard to believe that there could be so much trouble in the world on such a beautiful day.

Like the true blot on the landscape, the black cloud she could see hovering over Cherbourg brought home how close the war was to them and the desperate plight of millions of people across Europe.

Villacoublay, Paris, France.

Bernhard just had time to grab some food and a canteen full of water from his tent in their makeshift camp before running back to his plane for another mission.

The ground crew were frantically refuelling and re-arming the plane and he was soon taxiing back out on to the runway and taking off towards Cherbourg. It was his third mission that day. The French and British defence of the town was proving stubborn and as he flew low across the French countryside he could see columns of panzer tanks and troop-carrying trucks all heading towards the coast in the same direction he was flying.

Within the hour, the Kette of planes he was leading was approaching the ruined town of Cherbourg. The smoke from burning buildings marked the target for him but his brief orders were to concentrate his bombs on the harbour area. It was there that the French were putting up the sternest resistance while the British evacuated the last of their Expeditionary Force.

With little air defence left in the town, he flew low across the target to get a good look at what was happening, leading the three aircraft in a tight circle to watch the battle below.

The situation was too confused for him to be sure where the battle lines were drawn but he saw several small vessels against the piers and frantic activity around them, as a few remaining troops tried to embark and evacuate the town. They would be his target he decided and pulled away from the coast to prepare his bombing run.

After a quick exchange with Willie, who doubled up as their bomb aimer, they made their chosen approach and dropped their stack of 8 bombs all around the boats and the jetty. The results were devastating.

As with all pilots the immediate carnage of his work wasn't in plain sight as the explosions took place behind him. One of the two K's reported back that he had hit the target and as he circled around to look for himself, he saw the bombs of the third plane in the Kette explode on the jetty and around the flotilla of small boats.

He was surprised to see what looked like women and children lying amongst the debris and couldn't believe what they had just done. In fact, the harder he looked the more he realised there were few military vehicles or troops anywhere near the jetty they had attacked.

He couldn't afford to wait around any longer, more Heinkel's were approaching and his orders were to get back to base and refuel and re-arm again for further missions.

Just as he was about to call off the attack he spotted a barricade of vehicles in one area of the town and could see troops and guns firing towards the advancing panzers. Over the radio he told the two K's his plan and they flew low across the port, machine guns blazing away at the French defenders. He noted them scatter and some fell as they were attacked from behind by the Kette of Heinkel 111's. Kai and Karl shook hands in the fuselage of the Heinkel then started some good-natured arguing as to who had caused the most damage. Willie started laughing but Bernhard couldn't get the images of the women and children out of his head.

During the attack, a few brave souls at the barricade had turned to fire at the planes and one bullet had flown through the cockpit, entering through the glass at the bottom and passing between him and Willie then out through the glass roof. It had been a narrow escape.

He was a lucky pilot.

He was sure their attack had provided support for Rommel's 7th Armoured Division with their advance into the port and he was happy that they had made at least some positive contribution to the fight. They set off for Paris, Willie chattering with the two K's, but he couldn't join in as the dead civilians still haunted his thoughts.

He couldn't be sure it had been his bombs that had done the damage but he had chosen the target and felt responsible. He was devastated.

What he didn't know was that the last major evacuation of troops had been completed the day before and the only evacuation that was taking place were a few stragglers and desperate civilians trying to leave France for the safety of England.

Guernsey

By the time, Laurence caught the bus home his mind was firmly made up.

Rachel had to go to England with the school, that way at least one of them would be safe.

He was sure the school would look after Rachel well but what he couldn't get straight in his head was how he would persuade Rachel to leave her mum.

He read the paper on the way home as usual and noted that the island was officially demilitarized and he hoped that might secure their safety. But on the other hand, he knew now there would be no defence. Despite the war, holidays were still being promoted in Jersey and Sark, *now that would be nice* he thought. He had never been to either island.

The paper also reported that there would be no car driving at night and Le Riches had a display of things to eat on meatless days. *Things were getting tight*, he thought.

He also noted there had been a huge air raid on the east coast of England and there had been more air raids over Malta. The end of the war for France was expected today. He wondered how that might feel for the French people and what their future might hold. He then read the list of things Rachel should take when she was evacuated with the school. That brought him back to the enormity of the next 24 hours. With his practical head on he was sure they had everything she would need.

The family had an early tea of liver, boiled potatoes and cabbage. Rachel had been sent around the corner to Luff's for some biscuits and sweets before tea and had come home with some Bluebird Liquorice Toffees, one of the families favourites. They would enjoy a few of those before bed time. It was a lovely evening and as soon as the dishes were done Laurence suggested he and Lily go for a quick walk down to the beach. They crossed the road and took the few steps on to the pebbles opposite their house. They had left Rachel in charge, listening to Melody and Co on the Home Service on the radio, with strict instructions that they should only eat two toffees each.

They sat down on the pebbles and watched the tide slowly ebb away. Time seemed to stand still as the beauty of the moment transfixed them. A boat left the harbour of St Peter Port and a few sailing boats were enjoying a trip up and down the Little Russel, the three-mile-wide channel between Guernsey and Herm. He could see one fishing boat close in, pulling pots and hopefully collecting a good catch of crabs and lobsters. The seagulls circled the small boat looking for scraps as they always did. Looking north east, the smoke from Cherbourg seemed to be thinner now, the battle was probably over.

Laurence put his arm around Lily and she rested her head on his shoulder and started to gently weep. The moment she had been dreading all day had come.

'I have been thinking about this all afternoon my Love and I think Rachel should go with the school tomorrow.'

It had been said and he dreaded the reply. He was worried they might argue, something they never seemed to do.

To his surprise, she agreed.

'I know Laurie. I think that would be best for her,' she said quietly.

'I walked home today and all I could think of was doing all we can to keep Rachel safe. This is the best thing we can do for her.'

'And you my Love? What do you want to do?' Laurence asked her with a lot of trepidation.

'I'm staying with you and the little ones.' Lily said emphatically. 'I am not leaving you.'

Laurence pulled her close and they kissed.

'Guess we had best get things organized then,' he said.

He stood up, pulling his wife up from the pebbles. She dusted down her skirt and they crossed the road, hand in hand, to their home to put the plan into action.

Lily sat down with Rachel and told her she had to go to England with the school to be safe from the Germans, Rachel nodded taking it all in.

'You'll be there too Mummy?' she asked with a pleading look in her eye.

'No sweetie, I can't go. I have to stay here and look after your brother and sister.'

'Then I'll stay and help too. I'm not leaving you and going away on my own – never!'

The look of grim determination on her face would have been comical on one so young in any other circumstances but this was too serious for anyone to laugh.

The argument went on for some time and Lily was in tears for most of it as was Rachel. They finally called it a day and decided to let Rachel go to bed, she was exhausted from all the emotion.

Laurence slipped out while she was getting ready for bed to walk to the Parish Hall to see what was happening. The place was a hive of activity as plans were being made to cope with rationing, moving the school and air raid warnings. He got in a queue in front of a desk which had a sign marked EVACUATION on the wall above and behind it.

When it was his turn, Laurence registered Rachel to be evacuated with the school. At the point of writing her name on the list he hesitated, just for a second, but it had to be done and with the queue building behind him he wrote her name down and then put his name down for ARP duties. After picking up what information he could about the evacuation he headed back home.

He now knew that the plans were to keep the school together as much as possible and it was likely they would end up in Scotland or the far north of England. The boat would probably be heading for Weymouth on the south coast of England and they would then be going on by train.

He also knew that no-one would be allowed near the quay to see the boat off.

Laurence walked home, tears streaming down his face. The thought of losing Rachel, even for a day, was tearing him apart.

He was tempted to pop into the local pub as he walked passed but he never drank and now was not a good time to start. He did pause and looked through the window at the few customers who sat at the tables.

The place was thick with smoke and flat caps were the norm. He shook himself, splashed his face with water from a horse trough outside the pub, and walked quickly home to break the news.

Rachel and the other children were in bed and Laurence slipped in and gave them all a kiss goodnight on the forehead. Rachel was still awake, thinking about what had been said and obviously too emotionally shocked to sleep.

He sat on the edge of her bed and stroked her hair. 'You know I love you and always will.'

'I know Daddy,' she replied.

'Would you go tomorrow if Mummy was waiting for you at the other end of the boat journey.' Why he had said something so silly he wasn't sure, it had just popped into his head.

'Yes Daddy, I would. Can you do that?'

'Of course, we can arrange anything you like,' he lied.

Rachel beamed her big smile. 'I am excited now. I have never been on a big boat before. If there are some games to play I'll try and win a prize. Will that make you proud?'

'It will my darling daughter, Oh it will. I can't wait to hear all about it. Now get some sleep, it's an early start for you tomorrow. I need to sort out your Mum's trip to make sure she is waiting for you in England. Night, night.'

'Night, night Daddy,' Rachel replied in a sleepy voice

Laurence went back to Lily and as they sat down he told her what he had done.

'Do you think she really believes I'll be in England waiting for her?'

'I think she does,' he replied. 'I hated lying to her but I think it's the only way. Goodness knows what will happen when she gets to England and finds you're not there to meet her.'

There was a quiet knock on the front door.

Laurence got back up and answered the door. It was Ma and she was extremely upset.

She came in to tell them all the news she had heard from Cherbourg. She told of women being raped, men being shot at point blank range. Children were dying, hospitals were being destroyed and whole families were losing their lives.

Laurence thought the stories were probably exaggerated but they helped reinforce their decision to send Rachel to England.

Ma was upset by the news about Rachel but understood their reasons and agreed to help in any way she could.

'Well Ma, you can help me pack her things,' Lily said

Laurence got out the Star newspaper while Lily found Rachel a small bag. Between them they gathered the meager list of clothing and a few items of food.

One vest
One pair of knickers
One bodice
One petticoat
2 pairs of stockings
Handkerchiefs, lily packed three
A slip and a blouse
A cardigan
Night clothes
Comb, toothbrush, towel, soap, face-cloth, boots, shoes and plimsolls

The food she could take included sandwiches, egg or cheese, (no discussion needed, Rachel loved cheese sandwiches) nuts and raisins, dry biscuits, an apple and an orange and some barley sugar sweets. Everything on the list, except the orange as they didn't have one, were packed in a brown paper bag for Rachel to eat during the trip, Lily spread extra sweets, Liquorice Toffees, through Rachel's bag, each individually wrapped and hidden so that she would find them as a surprise.

She then got out Rachel's clothes for tomorrow and made sure her coat had a few more surprises in the pockets. She planned to make sure Rachel wore two pairs of knickers and an extra blouse. It was all she could think of to help her beloved daughter cope for goodness knows how long.

There were tears in her eyes as she folded and packed. Eventually she was happy with her work.

Ma popped into Rachel's bedroom and kissed the sleeping girl on the forehead before heading home.

Soon after Ma had left, Lily put on her dressing gown and snuggled next to Laurence on the sofa. Not even the sounds of the BBC Orchestra on the Home Service and later Big Bill Campbell and his Canadian Cowboys could put a smile on her face.

There would be no sleep for Lily and Laurence.

The night passed so slowly.

They talked intermittently through the night about the rights and wrongs of Rachel going on her own to England with the school. What would happen when they got to England? Where would the school end up? They had no answers.

If Laurence could have left, then they might have all made the journey but he couldn't because he was too old to join the army. Right now, it seemed logical that they stay in their house for as long as they could and keep most of the family together.

The clocks in the house ticked away, filling the silence. The decision stayed the same.

Villacoublay, Paris, France

After the three raids on Cherbourg in the morning, the rest of the day had been quiet. There had been a routine patrol around the coast for three crews from Kampfgeschwader 55, but the rest of the planes had been grounded. This was good news for the ground crews who finally had the chance to work on the planes and carry out much needed repairs.

Bernhard had not been required to fly after his attacks on Cherbourg, so had spent much of the day in a deck chair outside his temporary tented billet near the control tower. He watched the repair crews, with interest and curiosity, as they replaced the glass panels in the cockpit. They also patched a few holes in the wings that he hadn't noticed until they were pointed out to him by the *Unterfeldwebel* in charge of the maintenance work. *Lucky again*, he thought. Glad that the bullets hadn't hit anything vital.

A large black Labrador had adopted him almost as soon as he arrived at the base and now lay across his feet waiting for a walk or food. Bernhard read, or at least tried to read, a local paper, his French wasn't that great but he hoped by immersing himself in the local papers it would get better. He also had a few books he had brought with him from Germany that he could read when he needed a distraction. He kept a diary and religiously filled in all that happened each day but that task was left to last thing at night, before lights out.

He wasn't alone, about 20 other crewmen were lounging around in a similar manner. A few were tinkering with bits of kit and one pilot had taken his Luger to bits to clean it and was now struggling to put it back together. Several of his crew were laughing at his predicament which led to smiles all around.

Dozing next to him in his deckchair was Willie, his friend and navigator. Near the apron, the two K's kicked a ball to each other, hoping some of the others might join in for an impromptu football match. In the summer heat though, no-one else seemed inclined to vacate their deck chairs.

Others watched intently as the ground crews worked on their aircraft and occasionally they would walk over to check on progress or mention something that needed attention, if they could see it had been over-looked.

The afternoon wore on until just after 5pm. Bernhard had resigned himself to a no more flying that day. He could see the two K's, who had long given up their game, lying together on the grass staring up at the skies, chatting about who knew what. They seemed inseparable at times.

Suddenly a loud wailing noise burst into life just above them and people started to run in all directions to their emergency stations. The air raid siren meant they were under imminent attack. Gun crews were soon in place, several 88s, the anti-aircraft versions, had been positioned around the perimeter of the airfield in sand bag bunkers and machine gun crews were dotted around the base. Some were also positioned on the control tower roof above him.

The group's Major suddenly burst from the control tower and shouted for all the pilots to get their planes into the air if they could.

Bernhard grabbed his helmet, patted the Labrador on the head and ran for his Heinkel. It only took a few minutes but by the time the engines were starting the first Messerschmitts from Jagdgeschwader 26 were already off the ground to help defend the aerodrome against the British bombers and he could hear the first reports from the big 88s letting rip at the attackers.

He was proud that the two K's were with him, they had all sprinted to the plane at top speed and had got on board in a matter of minutes, but Willie had been inside the tower when the siren had sounded and hadn't made it to the plane.

Bernhard was desperate to get into the air and couldn't wait for the him. He knew he had to get away from the bombs that would soon be falling on Villacoublay.

He didn't pause at the end of the runway and started his take off run. He could see flak exploding in the sky up ahead and for a second thought he could see the planes high above him.

He was getting near take off speed when a stick of bombs exploded ahead of him. They fell in a line across the runway and he knew he would hit the debris but he ploughed on, he just hoped his Heinkel didn't drop into a crater. He also hoped lightning wouldn't strike twice and no more bombs would fall on that spot.

The plane went light as they left the ground just as he careered through the smoke and flying debris from the runway. A large bang suddenly rocked the plane and a piece of concrete smashed through the glass cockpit and fell into the seat where Willie would normally be sitting.

The rush of wind shocked him but he kept the throttles forward and pulled back on the stick as they came out of the smoke. He immediately veered to the right of the runway line and kept low to try and camouflage his plane against the countryside below.

He looked back but there was no-one following him.

It seemed as if he was the only Heinkel to take off.

Kai had taken the top gun spot and was ready to fire on any attackers but his guns remained silent as Bernhard pulled the wheels up and powered away from the airfield. It looked like the attack was a simple bombing raid without fighter support.

Checking the gauges, he noted he was light on fuel but he was OK for half an hour or so. Everything else seemed fine. He had watched the engineers working on his plane earlier in the day. The plane felt OK but the noise from the wind rushing through the hole in the cockpit was deafening. He didn't want to go too fast with that damage and he was worried there may have been more damage to other parts of the aircraft that he wasn't aware of.

He half smiled as he thought of the engineers replacing more glass in the cockpit and could hear their curses in his head.

He managed to signal Kai to come to him and he shouted over the noise that he would circle Paris before coming back to the airfield to check if the raid was over. He asked Kai to talk to Karl and between them try and see if he could spot any other damage to the bomber.

Kai clambered off to talk to Karl and to inspect the plane as best they could from the various vantage points offered by the gun turrets. All he could spot were a few rips in the starboard wing between the engine and the damaged cockpit. Nothing seemed too serious. He reported back to Bernhard, having to shout above the wind noise. There had been no time for the two K's to don their flying helmets and set up the on board wireless communication system.

Feeling safe, now he was away from the base, Bernhard circled the Heinkel away towards Paris.

The Eiffel Tower stood tall above the surrounding buildings and although Bernhard had seen it before he had never seen it this close from the air. He flew close by and Kai gave him the thumbs up as they enjoyed a wonderful view of Paris in the early evening light. A swastika waved proudly from the top of the tower.

Amazingly he could already see other red, black and white banners hanging from key buildings as a reminder to the locals that they were now under German control. He felt a moment of pride that they had captured such a great city with so little resistance.

He decided to swing back to Villacoublay as he was sure the raid must now be over. A few columns of smoke from damage on the ground gave him a clue as to the wind direction and he lined up on the runway. He could see that there was considerable damage to the runway itself so swung off to the right, choosing the line of least damage and landed his plane on the grass. Kai and Karl gave him the usual round of applause.

Heinkels were scattered around the airfield as crew had frantically tried to spread their planes apart to avoid the risk of giving the attackers a big target to aim at. In future, the planes would never be lined up together as they had been before the raid.

Two planes had been hit before they could be moved and lay in ruins. As an ambulance was alongside one he assumed one of the pilots had managed to get to the plane before it was hit.

As he taxied back towards the control tower, avoiding several craters on the way, Kai patted him on the back to point out that the Messerschmitt's they shared the airfield with were also landing.

Oberleutnant Holstein was waiting for him as the plane ground to a halt on the concrete stand in front of the tower. At least that seemed undamaged.

As the props stopped turning the Oberleutenant walked over and looked up through the hole in the damaged cockpit. 'Well done Bernhard', he shouted. 'I'll get the crew over to fix this as soon as we can. We need all the pilots we can get right now, especially ones who think and move as quickly as you.'

He gave a brief Hitler salute and walked off towards the ground crew who were gathered around the still smoldering wrecks. No doubt wondering what they could salvage.

Kai climbed alongside him, brushing concrete and glass off Willie's seat.

'Well Bernhard, that's a first.'

'What's that?' Bernhard replied.

'I have been in this squadron over a year now and that is the first time I have heard the Oberleutnant call anyone by their first name! I reckon there's a medal in this one for you.'

He shook Bernhard's hand and clambered back and out of the aircraft, closely followed by Karl.

Bernhard sat there for a moment, pondering how lucky he was that the piece of concrete hadn't been a metre to the right, trying not to imagine the damage it would have done if it had hit him.

He was brought back to reality by the smashing of glass and the sight of the crew clearing away the remaining jagged shards and getting ready to replace the damaged section.

He clambered back out of his seat and down the ladder out of the bottom of the plane and stood watching the maintenance crew work for a moment. They were all smiling and gave him the thumbs up.

'Time for a schnapps,' he muttered to himself and went off after Kai and Karl to find Willie.

As he walked back he noticed his hands were shaking but there was no time to rest and recover. Oberleutnant Holstein was waiting for him as he reached the tower and ushered him into the briefing room.
Soon he and Willie were sitting with two other crews learning about their next mission. It had been decided to raid the port of Weymouth that evening, as night descended. They were shown images of shipping in the harbour and these were the main target.

All too soon, Bernhard and Willie were back in their Heinkel, the glass in the canopy having been quickly replaced and the wings patched. Bernhard had been telling Willie about his lucky escape earlier in the day and Willie was grateful he hadn't been quick enough to get to the plane before Bernhard had taken off.

It was already getting dark as they took off to the west towards the setting sun. This time they would be hugging the sea as they headed west across France and then over the Channel. They passed close to Alderney before heading north towards the English coast. They kept to a maximum height of 200 metres until they crossed the coast over a sparsely populated area to the west of Lyme Regis. They then looped to their right gaining height to 500 metres, passing Axminster and travelling almost as far as Crewkerne before turning and heading back south towards Weymouth. No shots were fired and none of the crew saw any enemy planes in the failing light. Their view ahead in the half-light was perfect as they kept the arrow like line of the Chesil beach to their right.

As they neared their target, they dropped back down to 200 metres and they could see Weymouth and the harbour set out in front of them.

As planned, the Kette of three Heinkel 111's lined up in formation and flew quickly across the harbour, dropping their bomb loads as they went.

Bernhard was on the left of the formation and while the others sped for home he peeled left and went back to see what damage they had caused. He gave the town a wide berth as some anti-aircraft fire and search lights were now criss-crossing the sky above the harbour. He couldn't make out any damage in the darkness but he felt sure they had hit at least one vessel.

He made a mental note of where the anti-aircraft fire was coming from and followed the rest of his Kette back to Villacoublay in the gathering darkness.

A flare signaled them in and they landed by the light of barrels full of burning wood, lined up on each side of the runway.

Once again, the crew applauded the landing and they ran towards de-briefing to get that over with as quickly as possible.

It had been a long day and Bernhard couldn't wait to get this down in his diary, and even more so, get some decent sleep.

Chapter 2 – Thursday 20th June 1940

In the News

Germans capture Lyons
First Anzac Troops arrive in the UK
Comedian Charley Chase dies in America

The small alarm clock next to Laurence rang loudly, waking him with a start. He must have dropped off to sleep eventually. When he turned over Lily was already up.

It was 6am and it was time to get up even though he felt shattered after a restless night. This would be a tough day.

Lily had got up before the alarm and had already placed Rachel's small case by the front door, ready for her 'big adventure'.

Laurence got dressed quickly after washing his face in the bowl that sat on the dressing table, and sneaked quietly into the lounge. He got out a writing set and sat down in the peace and quiet of the lounge to write a letter, the toughest he had ever written. In his elegant hand writing, but with a shaking hand, he wrote to his eldest daughter.

It explained about the evacuation, how it might be some time before they saw her again. It gave their address so she could write and tell them where she was staying and above all it told her just how much they loved her. He explained how they had decided she should go to England to keep her safe from a possible German invasion of Guernsey. He included a precious English pound note in the envelope and sealed it tight.

While Lily was preparing breakfast, he opened the case and hid the letter under her clothes.

Once that was done he went into the kitchen and gave Lily a huge hug. The kettle was whistling on the aga, ready for the first cup of cha, or Rosy Lee as Laurence often called it, of the day.

Lily went upstairs to wake Rachel from her sleep.

She was up like a shot, excited about the day ahead.

While she was eating, Lily stole away to the lounge and she too put pen to paper. Tears filling her eyes as she wrote a quick note in her unsteady hand. She wrapped it around a sweet and slipped it deep into Rachel's coat pocket beneath a handkerchief.

Washed and fed, Lily took some time plaiting Rachel's long black hair, while they waited for Ma to appear. Once Ma arrived, they left Laura and Michael with her and after the goodbyes the three of them walked hand in hand up to the school. As they walked the misty early morning clouds were burning away and the sunshine started to push through. It would be a beautiful but painful morning.

As they walked, Rachel asked questions about the boat, the trip and where she was going and in that universal way of parents the world over they replied without really saying anything – after all they didn't know any of the answers. They arrived at the school and the playground was already a hive of activity.

Outside of the school several buses were waiting to take the children to the boat. Some were already full and had their engines running. They went into the school hall and confirmed Rachel was here for the trip, her name being ticked off on the lengthy list. She was given a label with her name and school written on it and Lily attached it to the top button hole of her coat. She was also given a gas mask in a cardboard box which she placed over her head and under her arm like a small handbag.

'What's this for?' Rachel asked her Dad.

'It's just a safety mask for you on the boat,' he replied in a matter of fact way. 'You need one to be able to go on the boat these days.'

Rachel seemed to accept that and smiled trustingly at her parents. Lily smiled back, fighting the urge to cry.

Lily and Rachel hugged and for a while it seemed as if Lily would never let her go. Laurence put his arms around them both and after what seemed an eternity told them it was time for Rachel to get on the bus.

'Enjoy the trip my beauty.' Lily told her daughter. 'See you in England.'

'I will, see you later,' she replied.

Rachel turned and ran for the bus, waving as she ran.

Lily and Laurence joined the other parents as the buses started up, belching black diesel fumes as they coughed into life. They smiled and waved and many of the children waved back. They could see Rachel in the window with one of her school friends. Several teachers were also with them, standing in the aisles making sure everyone was behaving. With much crunching of gears and smoke, the buses turned around in the playground and headed for the road.

As the last of the buses turned the corner a collective moan went up and many started to cry. Laurence and Lily hugged as did many other couples. They both cried.

Eventually they parted and walked slowly home, Lily linked arms with Laurence and rested her head against his shoulder, nothing was said. Both could only think of their daughter taking the boat on her own to who knows where and how she would react when she realised she was on her own. Who knew when they would see her again? Who knew if they would ever see her again? Neither of them would speak that thought.

When they got home they sat Laura and Michael down and told them the news. Both cried when they realised Rachel would not be coming home that night.

Michael's tears stopped quickly but Laura seemed to take it more to heart and was inconsolable. There was no point hiding the truth from them, who knew when they would all be together again.

Michael didn't really understand what had happened. He would ask several times where Rachel was before he got it straight in his head that she had gone away.

Laurence took the 8.30 bus to work, he was late but that wasn't uppermost in his mind. He walked down the jetty to his office and could see the school children queuing to get on the boat. There was also a queue of children and parents all the way down the quay and up St Julian's Avenue. In fact, as he looked back he couldn't see the end of the queue.

There must be thousands of people leaving, he thought.

He noted the boat that the children were currently boarding was the SS Whitstable.

Other boats were already leaving the island and more were waiting to dock.

At least the Whitstable looked in reasonable condition, he thought, as others seemed to be nothing more than freighters. One naval vessel was also being pressed into service in support of the evacuation. In all 25 ships took part in the evacuation that day.

He made his way up to the jetty roof and watched them all getting on board but couldn't see Rachel amongst the mass of children. He realised there was no sign of the buses that had taken the children from the school so she could have already left the island. He had hoped for one last sight of her but soon realised that was not to be.

Somewhere in the crowd Rachel held on to her friend for dear life and as they were hustled and bustled towards the boat. She kept looking round to see if she could see her Mum or Dad but with all of the teachers, parents and other children around her she couldn't see anything apart from the sky above. Suddenly she was on to the gangplank and virtually pushed on to the boat.

She was ushered into the interior of the boat and from there could see very little of Guernsey from her seat in the middle of the main cabin.

She was lucky to have a seat as many were standing or trying to sit in the aisles. She didn't like the smell. It was sweaty and uncomfortable being so hemmed in. *I hope I don't need the toilet*, she thought, wishing immediately she hadn't had that thought.

Reluctantly Laurence returned to the office. A strong cup of tea and a biscuit was waiting on his desk. Agnes, his secretary looked up and smiled and he mouthed a thank you back. No-one mentioned what time it was.

Outside his window the boat was soon fully loaded and making its way out of the harbour. Another boat quickly took its place as more buses arrived from other schools and more children piled out ready to make their way up the gang planks.

On the sight of the boat leaving, Laurence answered the parental call and quickly made his way back up to the roof and watched the SS Whitstable sail past Castle Cornet and head north towards England and safety. A group of parents had made their way to the Castle Lighthouse at the end of the jetty and were waving to the boat as it steamed out of the harbour. Children lined the railings waving back, looking for one last glimpse of their parents. Laurence could hear the cheering from where he stood.

He stayed there for a full ten minutes as he watched the SS Whitstable pass Brehon Tower. In the distance, he noticed a black cloud of smoke rising high into the sky from the direction of Cherbourg. What he didn't know was that the docks were being destroyed by the British army and navy personnel to avoid them being used by the Germans.

He didn't dwell on the smoke as, for better or worse, Rachel was on her way. As he cast one last look at the SS Whitstable, he just hoped and prayed that the boats all got to England safely.

On the boat, Rachel had felt a little relief as many had tried to get outside and take one last look at Guernsey. She took the chance to pop to the toilet and was shocked at the state of it already. She certainly hoped she didn't need to go again. As she walked back to her seat she could see they were already out of the harbour and heading towards England. Brehon Tower slipped past, she had never seen it so close and was impressed at how big it was. Children, teachers and parents made their way back to their seats as the island disappeared behind them.

The majority of Guernsey's young generation were heading into the unknown.

Rachel guessed there would be no games on this boat, there being so many people on board, but she was happy. After all she was on an adventure and her Mum would be waiting for her in England.

While Rachel was starting her journey, Lily, Ma and the children crossed the road and sat on one of the seats opposite the halfway and watched as the boats sailed by. Lily didn't know which one Rachel was on but she waved to each boat in turn as they sailed away. She knew in her heart that even if Rachel had been standing on the side of the boat and looking their way, she wouldn't have seen them, but she felt it was something she had to do.

Meanwhile in St Peter Port, other boats came and went and tomatoes were still being shipped in huge numbers. The Star recorded the numbers and reported that nearly 100,000 chip baskets were being sent daily.

Time passed and before Laurence realised it, the day had gone and everyone started to pack up and go home. He put on his jacket and headed down the jetty. There were no children left waiting for evacuation and the harbour was empty apart from one small freighter loading up with the last of the day's tomato crop.

A lone small knitted teddy lay in the gutter on the quay side amongst the debris left by the crowd, a sad reminder of the children who had sailed away that day. He picked it up, absentmindedly stroked its head and without thinking put it in his jacket pocket.

He paid his penny for the paper and noted the headline "No Cause for Panic". It referred to the run on the banks and how the amount you could withdraw at any one time had been limited. *I wish I had some money I could take out,* he thought.

He folded the paper under his arm and headed home, he decided to walk this time. As he walked his mind was in turmoil. Had they done the right thing? Where was Rachel now? Had her boat been attacked on the way to England?

All of these questions distracted him from the view and the steady traffic that passed him as people headed home from town.

He wasn't alone on his walk as the good weather ensured most people walked to avoid paying for the bus. He occasionally looked at the paper and one of the headlines reminded him of his predicament. It was official, only men of military age could leave the island. That meant he was stuck in Guernsey. Lily, Laura and Michael could leave, but he wouldn't be allowed on the boat.

He knew from the schedules he saw that there weren't that many boats leaving now. The main evacuation was complete so apart from the mail boat and the tomato and freight boats, that would be it. *Have we missed the chance to get them away,* he thought?

As they prepared tea that night the mood was somber. It was liver again as food was beginning to be in short supply in some shops and meals were likely to get repetitive. No-one dared say anything, the mood could easily turn to tears if any criticism or argument had been made. Lily tried to lift the mood by asking Laurence about his day and he, quickly realising what was happening, picked up on her cue and reached for his jacket pocket, producing the small teddy. He gave it to Michael, who was suddenly all smiles. Even Laura picked up on the mood and put her hand on her father's hand and smiled up at him. He leant over and kissed her on the head.

Laura and Michael were missing Rachel but not as much as Lily. No helper at tea time and a spare pinny on the back of the door had caused several tears already. The empty chair did not help. Laurence made a mental note to put that in the shed before breakfast next morning.

After tea, which finished with a wonderful rice pudding, the kids were sent out in the yard to play and Lily told Laurence about her day.

Once they had tired of waving at the boats, and Ma had taken Laura and Michael to her house, Lily had gone out to her work. She was a house cleaner for a couple of Guernsey families and had gone to her first job at around 11am. She had knocked on the door but didn't get an answer. The key wasn't under the mat either.

The family had two young boys and Lily concluded they must have decided to evacuate, leaving the island with their children.

As there had been no work to do she had gone to the second house and this time the door was unlocked.

She had found a note on the hall table addressed to her to tell her that she was no longer required. It had included a week's wages in lieu of notice, a precious 10 shillings. Their children had also been evacuated and as the house was hardly being used her services were not needed. As a result Lily was now out of work and would need to look for something else to do to help them earn enough to keep the house running.

Laurence smiled and pointed out that with so many people leaving there would be plenty of work. In fact, the paper was full of stories of people needed to work in the vineries (greenhouses), growing and packing tomatoes. Many shops and other businesses were appealing for staff too.

After supper Laura picked out one of her reading books and sat next to her father, flicking through the pages. Michael was still awake, sitting in Rachel's place hugging his new Teddy, taking it all in but understanding little. Laurence got out his paper and they sat like that with barely a word spoken for almost an hour. Lily was in the kitchen tidying up after tea and sorting out the dishes. He saw her go out to water her tomatoes and do some washing.

There was little to be positive about in the paper. He read the article in detail about the run on the banks and the appeal for people not to panic. That made him think how the island's economy would fare with so much money going out with the people that were leaving. More unnerving was the headline that there had been more air raids in England overnight, one over Weymouth. What had they done sending Rachel there? It was so peaceful in the island now.

Ma had popped around during the evening to see how they all were and help Lily get Laura and Michael ready for bed. While that was happening, Laurence distracted himself by thumbing through some music scores he had been given. Although he knew there would be no dance that Saturday he hoped the ban wouldn't be for long. Anyway, it gave him something else to think about. He closed his eyes and in his mind played along on his drums with the music in his head, absentmindedly tapping away at the arms of his chair.

Michael and Laura came back in to kiss their father goodnight, disturbing him from his reverie. They had an extra-long cuddle before they went to bed.

Once the children were asleep and Ma had gone home, he and Lily settled down for the evening with a cup of tea. He got out the paper again and noted that with many of the men going off to fight it was also announced that all senior football was being suspended.

Won't be going to watch a match this weekend, he thought. He was amazed at how normal most of the paper seemed. The usual adverts, the births and deaths, trivial news about people being drunk and disorderly. Life, overall, seemed to be going on just as it always had.

Motor House had a Morris Coupe for sale for the princely price of £7 and 10 shillings. For a moment, he could picture them all driving around the island and picnicking on the beach, then driving back home. All of them being the five of them. That thought brought tears to his eyes and he hid behind the paper so Lily wouldn't see the tears running down his face.

As always, the conversation, when they were alone, moved back to the war and how long ot would go on for. They also talked about Rachel's journey.

'How long do you think it takes to get to England?' Lily asked Laurence.

'I'm not sure dear,' Laurence answered honestly. 'It depends how fast the boat goes, maybe 5 or 6 hours he suggested'.

'That means she will be there now. I wonder if she read my note?' Lily said, as if to the empty room.

Laurence looked surprised.

'You left her a note too?' Laurence replied. 'I hid mine in her case.'

'Mine's in her coat pocket.' Lily said smiling.

They had a little laugh at that, they thought so much alike at times.

'I wonder how she was when I wasn't there to meet her?' Lily asked.

'I am sure she was fine.' Laurence replied, seeking to reassure his wife.

This brought a few more tears from Lily.

Having had enough of the war, the Germans and the evacuation, they spent the rest of the evening talking about the weekend and when his next performance at St Georges Hall might be.

That was until 9.20pm when the War Commentary came on the Radio with news from the Home Service. There were more bombing raids in the home counties and discussions were still progressing on the French armistice. There never seemed to be any good news.

After the War Commentary, Jimmy Jewel and Jon Pertwee barely raised a smile from the Dodsworths as Up the Pole came on before bedtime. The radio was eventually switched off and a Glenn Miller record was played until black out time at 10.15.

Bed seemed a welcome relief after such an awful day. The young couple cuddled together and for a short while talked about Rachel and how she might be getting on. The reports on the radio of raids on England made them nervous about their decision. The chance that Rachel may have been caught up in a raid scared them deeply but neither of them really wanted to discuss that prospect.

There was little news relating to the Weymouth area nor anything about vessels being attacked so they pinned their hopes on the 'No News is Good New' maxim.

It was after midnight before sleep claimed Lily and longer still before Lawrence succumbed to the overwhelming tiredness he felt.

He just couldn't get Rachel out of his mind and when they might see her again. Tears were filling his eyes as he too eventually fell asleep.

Villacoublay, Paris, France

It had been a quiet start to the day for Kampfgeschwader 55. Bernhard had assumed his position in his deckchair early in the morning and, as usual, his new friend was curled up around his feet. He was reading the latest edition of Signal Magazine which kept him up to date with the progress of the war, he had given up on learning French for the time being.

The cover featured German Fallschirmjäger (paratroopers) and he wondered how long he would have to wait to see a picture of his Heinkel flying past the Eiffel Tower. He smiled at the thought. His family would be so proud.

Morning briefing had warned of a few potential raids on England but apart from being operationally ready he was still awaiting news of the action to come.

Out on the airfield the ground crews and engineers were working, as they had been all night, to make the airfield ready following the damage caused by the bombs dropped by the British, the day before. He had watched several fighters take off and land to test the runway and ensure all was well. The Messerschmitts were agile aircraft and he was sure they could take off and land on almost any surface. He hoped the patches on the concrete strip would be well and truly set before he had to take off with a full bomb load.

It was just after lunch, in fact he hadn't finished his coffee yet, when he was ordered to go to the briefing room with two other crews. 'Action at last, ' he muttered to himself.

Oberleutnant Holstein had a map of the English Channel on the wall. RAF bases on the south coast were marked with coloured pins, as were the Luftwaffe bases in northern France.

Some flags on the map showed raids in progress that day from other bases and he noted that the English airports were again under pressure. The main English harbours and shipping routes were also marked and the Oberleutnant told the three crews of his Kette that these were his target for that day.

He was to fly north from Paris, leading the Kette across the coast of France, before heading to the Isle of Wight then swinging west down the Channel hugging the English coast looking for targets of opportunity. He was then ordered to swing south and overfly Guernsey and Jersey to look out for any military activity before returning to base.

The crews walked out of the briefing room and headed out to their waiting planes. Bernhard called the crews over to him and gave them a short talk.

'Let's keep close today and everyone keep a good lookout for fighters. We'll keep a bit lower than instructed to try and keep out of sight of the English radar - follow my lead. I want us all back here in a couple of hours, no heroics.'

Bernhard shook hands with the pilots and all of the crew from the two-other aircraft and then they split up, each crew heading to their own Heinkel. He looked at the red Greif (Griffin) badge on the fuselage with its black wings and felt a moment of intense pride.

Bernhard looked around and noticed his new doggy friend had walked out with them to the edge of the apron. He thought for a moment and decided to call the dog Greif after their unit badge. He took a moment to pat Greif on the head and thought it was a great name for the faithful dog. He bent down and ruffled Greif's ear and then sent him back to the empty deckchairs. Greif drooped his head and sidled back, as instructed. Bernhard strapped on his helmet and with Willie and his crew walked out to his Heinkel 111.

He walked around the plane on his own giving it a visual check, then kicked the tyres, as he always did before a mission, while the rest of the crew climbed on board. He was always the last to climb on board and the last to leave the plane.

He went through a brief system check, he trusted his engineers, checked that his wireless radio link with the crew was working, checking in with each in turn, fired up the engines and taxied out to the runway. The wind was coming from its usual direction for this time of year so they lined up to take off to the west.

As they sat waiting, Bernhard noticed Willie was shifting around in his seat.

'What's up Willie?' Bernhard asked.

'I think I'm sitting on some glass,' he answered, shifting around again.

'Just think Willie, if you cut your ass on that glass you may just get a medal for injuries received while on a mission.'

The crew all laughed at that and were still laughing as the flare went up from the tower and Bernhard pushed the throttles forward.

Soon they were speeding past the maintenance crews who were still working on repairs around the aerodrome. He had a full set of eight bombs on board and the machine guns were fully armed.

The Heinkel 111 lifted off the runway and cleared the trees of the airport perimeter by around 20 metres. Bernhard banked to the right heading off towards the Channel.

They crossed over Versailles with Paris off to their right and after passing close to Rouen flew over Dieppe as they headed across the Channel.

Swinging to the left as they approached the English coast they dropped to 600 metres, as they searched for allied shipping. Kai, who had taken the top gunner role kept a lookout for the dreaded English fighters and reported that the two other crews were keeping close order. On such a clear day, they were always in danger of being attacked out of the sun, but for now the sky was clear.

Soon they spotted a lone coaster heading towards the Solent and Bernhard led the Kette of Heinkel 111s on an attack run. He dropped 4 bombs as did the other two planes but somehow, they all missed.

'Well that must have scared him!' said Willie, just a little too sarcastically for Bernhard's liking.

'You're the bomb aimer,' he replied. 'Maybe you need glasses, eh!'

Bernhard smiled at his close friend and they both burst out laughing.

They turned and attacked again this time just using their guns. A lone gun on the coaster started firing back and a near miss on one of the other planes was enough for Bernhard to call off the attack. He also knew they were in full view of the south coast so a call was probably on its way to one of the nearby fighter bases.

They hurried off continuing west, passing Bournemouth and its distinctive pier, and headed down towards Exeter.

'We'll get him another day!' laughed Willie as they headed away.

Another small coaster soon came into view. It looked like it was heading towards Weymouth. Once again Bernhard lined up for an attack. Diving down to 300 metres he lined up on the small vessel and was about to drop his remaining bombs when a small white flag on the mast caught his attention.

"Call off the attack!" he ordered as he flew low across the boat. A red cross flag was flying from the mast and he could see the decks were full of children. Some even waved as they flew by.

Quickly banking to the left he saw that the other two planes had followed suit. He wiped away a bead of sweat that was rolling down the side of his face and turned to Willie.

"That was close, I hate to think what would have happened if we had sunk a boat full of children!"

Willie nodded in agreement as the plane flew south, following the direction the boat had come from.

Ahead Bernhard could see the Channel Islands and he realised the islands were sending their children away, probably anticipating an invasion. Several other ships were following the same route and he steered clear of all of them.

Flying down the east coast of Guernsey he saw no evidence of military activity. There were rows of trucks lined up near the harbour and a lot of activity in the harbour itself but no shots were fired at him and he couldn't tell from his viewpoint what the trucks were doing.

He then flew across to Jersey and again was unchallenged as he crossed the coast and flew across the island. The harbour looked busy too but seemed a lot smaller than Guernsey's and didn't have the same trucks all lined up.

Fuel was getting low so he headed back across the coast of France and made his way back to Villacoublay.

Again, he led his Kette in a loop around Paris, marveling at the great metropolis that was now in German hands.

71

Landing to the usual applause from the crew he headed for debriefing and a well-earned mug of coffee. He would enjoy a schnapps later and would sleep well knowing he hadn't killed anyone today, especially a boat full of children.

Weymouth

As the boat docked in Weymouth late in the afternoon, Rachel was out of her seat and hugging the rails for signs of her mother. As they had sailed into the harbour, she had spotted several half sunken wrecks and the boat had been forced to weave its way to the quayside.

She had noticed that several of children had their mothers with them and when she had told them that her mum would be waiting for her in England they had just smiled, in that strange knowing way adults often had.

She stuck close to two of her closest friends from school who were also on their own. Julie, Christine and Rachel, the three musketeers, always together, always looking after each other.

As Rachel scoured the docks from the boat, there was no sign of her Mum and reluctantly with her bag in hand she had climbed down the gangway with her school friends and headed towards the waiting train. As she got nearer one of her teachers saw how distracted she was and asked her why.

'I am looking for my Mum Miss,' she replied.

'She won't be here Rachel, she is in Guernsey. I saw her when we were leaving on the bus.'

'But she promised she would be in England waiting for me, my Dad arranged it.'

'Impossible said the teacher. No other boats have made the journey this morning and no planes are flying. Now get on the train like a good girl so we can all go to our new school.'

'No!' screamed Rachel. 'I am going home to be with my Mum.'

'No, you are not young lady, now get on the train with the others.'

'No!' Rachel screamed again and made a bolt back towards the boat. A soldier caught her arm as she ran past him and dragged her to an abrupt halt. 'Now where do you think you're going,' he said in a strong Welsh accent that Rachel hadn't heard before.

That made Rachel scream even more and she started flailing her arms about in a real panic trying to get away. By now her frantic teacher had arrived and with the help of the soldier and one of his colleagues they physically carried Rachel, kicking and screaming on to the train.

As suddenly as they arrived and with no-one to wave goodbye to, the train full of Guernsey children left the station heading north into the gathering gloom.

A tearful Rachel sat huddled in one of the compartments with a teacher alongside her. She put her hand in her pocket for a handkerchief and pulled out a piece paper wrapped around a sweet. She unwrapped the paper and saw a note written in her Mum's uncertain handwriting. It read:

Dear Rachel

I am so sorry we had to lie to you. We knew you wouldn't go if I couldn't go too. I need to stay and look after Laura and Michael but we wanted you to be safe. The Germans might come here and we wanted to keep you safe from all of that. We will meet again real soon my Angel.

Be careful and be good.

Love you
A la perchoine

Mum, Dad, Laura and Michael xxxx

Rachel cried and cried until there were no more tears.

Eventually her eyes grew heavy, the hypnotic sound of the train travelling along the rails helped her fall asleep. In the darkness the three girls slept, huddled together in a corner of the carriage, the train taking them as far away from the war as possible.

Neither knew it then but it would be several years before Mother and Daughter were to be re-united.

Today would be a day Rachel would never forget.

Villacoublay, Paris, France

There would be no rest for Bernhard. Even as they had walked across the apron to their de-briefing their planes were being re-armed. The Oberleutnant was almost dismissive of their report and impatiently hurried them along before announcing they had another mission that evening. The map on the wall showed that Southampton was to be the target and it would be a 12 Heinkel raid, with Bernhard leading the mission at the head of his own Kette.

By 7pm they were back on the tarmac, tyres had been kicked and hands had been shaken, this time it was just with the pilots as he explained how they would hold formation on him and follow his lead as they attacked from the north. There were just too many men waiting to take off for him to talk to everyone.

Without realising it, he was becoming a veteran and a leader.

With 11 Heinkel's behind him they waited for the flare before taking off and circling over Paris as the crews got into position around him. A Gruppe of Messerschmitt 109's took up position high above them as they headed out towards the English Channel. They crossed the English coast, just west of Brighton, flying low at around 500 metres with the setting sun away to their left. They started to turn before Winchester and headed south, back towards Southampton. The tell-tale sight of the River Itchen and Southampton water lay ahead.

They could see the docks clearly and Willie guided him in from the bomb aimers position. At the right moment, he gave the signal and Bernhard reached up and pulled the bomb release. As he dropped his bombs the other 11 planes dropped their bombs too and a rain of destruction headed down and exploded in and around the docks.

He turned and got thumbs up from the K's as they could see the results of the attack.

Relieved of the weight of the bombs he could feel the Heinkel buck in his hands as it tried to gain height. However he did the opposite and used the increased agility of his plane to dive lower, crossing the Isle of Wight, before heading back to France and home, as fast as he could.

As agreed the other pilots followed suit but they broke formation and headed home independently. He was conscious that they had seen some flak but he had not heard any reports of any losses amongst his colleagues. The Messerschmitt 109's were waiting for them and raced past to head off any British fighters that might be pursuing them. He was amazed that they hadn't seen any Hurricanes or Spitfires.

It seemed they had the element of surprise. Lucky Bernhard had been lucky again.

He smiled as they crossed the French coast and headed back towards Paris.

Suddenly above the engine noise he was aware that Willie was singing Erika. Without thinking he joined in and soon the K's were singing along too.

'On the heath a little flower blooms, boom, boom, boom, And it's called, boom, boom, boom, Erika, boom, boom, boom Hot from a hundred thousand little bees, boom, boom, boom, that swarm over, boom, boom, boom, Erika, boom, boom, boom.
Because her heart is full of sweetness, boom, boom, boom Her flowery dress gives off a delicate scent, boom, boom, boom On the heath a little flower blooms, boom, boom, boom, And it's called, boom, boom, boom, Erika, boom, boom, boom Back at home lives a little girl, boom, boom, boom, and she is called, boom, boom, boom, Erika, boom, boom, boom This girl is my faithful darling, boom, boom, boom and my happiness, boom, boom, boom, Erika, boom, boom, boom When the flowers on the heath bloom red-lilac, boom, boom, boom, I sing this song to greet her, boom, boom, boom On the heath a little flower blooms, boom, boom, boom, And it's called, boom, boom, boom, Erika.'

With each boom, boom, boom they all thumped a piece of kit to make the noise of the drums, Bernhard making the sound rather than risk hitting anything sensitive.

After several stirring renditions, they were soon approaching the airfield so Bernhard reluctantly ordered the crew back to their stations as they made their approach. These guys were his family. *This was why he was a bomber pilot*, he thought. *You wouldn't get this type of camaraderie amongst the fighter boys.*

They landed to the obligatory round of applause and taxied across to the apron where the maintenance crews were waiting.

Bernhard was last out of the plane as always as he made sure everything was in order. He spoke to the maintenance crew while Willie waited and then they headed off for de-briefing, smiling and joking as they went. The rest of the Heinkel's were landing behind him as he walked over to the tower. Greif ran out to meet him.

He was sitting in the de-briefing room when the Oberleutnant came in and told him only 11 planes had returned. Freddie was missing. He asked permission to go up to the roof and without waiting for an answer, ran up to the balcony around the control tower. It was almost dark now but he still scoured the sky for any sign of a plane. But the night was quiet. He stood there for half an hour before Willie joined him and persuaded him to come down.

Freddie had been with them since Poland and was one of the original crews of Kampfgeschwader 55. He was a few days younger than Bernhard and while he wouldn't call him a close friend, they had shared many a drink together and some laughs too.

No-one knew what had happened to him and they hadn't received any reports of an aircraft being seen in trouble.

After de-briefing the pilots gathered together in the Officer's mess and toasted Freddie, wishing him a safe landing. The joy of the return to base had been instantly lost.

Bernhard headed off to get some sleep. *How could a plane just disappear?* He thought. Not knowing what had happened seemed even worse than knowing they had bailed out or crashed.

Writing about the loss in his diary made things worse and it took him a while to get to sleep that night.

Chapter 3 – Friday 21ˢᵗ June 1940

In the News

American radio broadcasts details of France's capitulation to Germany
General Wilhelm Keitel presents terms of surrender to French
Italians attack France in the Alps
"Peace" negotiations begin in France

Guernsey

Laurence and Lily were tired, the emotion of the day before had been draining, but life went on and work had to be done. Laurence's old alarm roused them from their sleep at 6.30am, and they all enjoyed a fried egg on toast for breakfast.

After an emotional send off from the family, Laurence was soon off to work on the morning bus. Ma popped around as usual but with no school and more importantly, no Rachel, Lily seemed lost and the house seemed very quiet.

To try and lift the mood Ma decided they should all have a treat and suggested they should head off to the Bridge in search of ice-cream.

Lily smiled as she thought of how tough her mother was and wished she could be like her. She knew she would need to be strong to get through the trials that seemed to be looming in their imminent future. She was often amazed at how Ma had coped with the loss of her husband, Lily's father. They rarely discussed it but Lily still remembered the day they were told Pa had died and how it happened.

Dozens of local families had been devastated that same day when the news arrived in the Island that the Germans had gassed the Guernsey Militia in their trenches.

They had set off, as had many other regiments of pals, full of hope and ready to deal with the Bosch. Lily remembered being at the harbour when the troops had marched off to war. The pals had been all smiles and looked strong and unbeatable. The last image she had of her Pa was him with his rifle slung across his back, marching past and waving to her and Ma.

Lily and her mother had been waving their handkerchiefs that day as did many of the other wives, mothers and children. It had felt like a celebration. In hindsight, there had been nothing to celebrate. The whole episode was a tragedy of epic proportions for the island and she never saw her father again. After the war ended it had been decided that the Guernsey militia should never fight as a unit to avoid the possibility of so many pals dying together and causing such damage to the community.

His photo, in which he stood proudly wearing his new uniform, sat on the mantelpiece above the fireplace in Lily's lounge. He smiled at her every time she entered the room and she always smiled back. Ma had the same photo next to her bed and Lily knew Ma often spoke to him before she went to sleep. *'Maybe that's how she keeps her strength,'* she thought.

Now it was all happening again, and Lily knew many more young men would die before this war was finally over.

"Blow it," she thought, let's all have some fun. There was little for the children to do in the house so they had to get out anyway. The idea of ice-cream had both kids smiling and jumping for joy and she had almost forgotten how beautiful Laura was when she smiled.

"Come on, let's go get ice cream," she announced, and soon they were off on their way to the Bridge. Michael half dragging Ma and Laura skipping along next to her mum. For a while they would put the war behind them and pretend all was well in the world.

On the bus, Laurence was deep in thought. He realised it was the summer solstice and from here on in the days would shorten on the way to December and Christmas. The realization suddenly shocked him, *what would they be doing this Christmas*? His eyes welled up as the idea of them not being all together for Christmas filled his head. He loved Christmas and the opportunity to have his family all around him for a whole day. They would religiously save money in the run up to Christmas and there was always a turkey on the table and presents under the tree.

He had often said to Lily that Christmas was what they worked for. To give the children the best presents they could afford and have a truly festive time. Memories of making decorations, finding oranges for the kid's stockings and telling tales of Santa's visit, brought tears to his eyes. He concentrated on looking out of the window in the hope no-one else would notice.

'*Perhaps it would be all over by Christmas*', he thought to himself. Trying to convince himself of that possibility. But he remembered the first world war and how everyone thought that would be over quickly. '*I hope we don't have to go through another 5 years of hell like last time*,' he thought. *Surely the human race can't be that stupid.*

The sea between Guernsey and Herm was flat calm and the sun, already high in the sky, reflected on the water, giving it that shimmer which looked so amazing no matter how many times you saw it. Sark, further away, had a sort of mirage effect going on with some of the island looking like it was suspended above the water.

He took this all in absentmindedly, as he was still thinking about what would happen in the next few months in the run up to Christmas. Before he knew it, the bus pulled up across the road from the Royal Hotel.

He and several others got off and walked off to their respective destinations. Laurence started walking to the office, dabbing his eyes with his neatly ironed hankie as he went. Today he ignored the drivers all lined up with their trucks full of tomatoes and walked down the other side of the road deep in thought. Amazingly the quay was covered in debris.

He realised it had been left by the thousands of people that had been evacuated from the island over the last couple of days. He didn't know the exact figure but the papers reported later that over 10,000 people had already left the island.

Several of the lorry drivers recognised him as he walked down the quay, but no-one called out to him. Many of them were also deep in thought and had worries of their own. Some of their friends had left and there were a few new faces amongst them, getting used to the routine of delivering their loads and the waiting that was involved.

Only the seagulls seemed unperturbed. Many were on the quay picking at the odd sandwich that had been dropped the day before. Others wheeled about following a fishing boat that was just coming back from an early morning outing with what must have been a good catch.

Laurence felt a type of desolation, it was as if something vital had changed in his island home. It wasn't just the loss of Rachel but something even deeper. It seemed that the heart was being ripped out of Guernsey and something terrible was about to happen.

Villacoublay, Paris, France

Although it was early in the morning the airport was a hive of activity as the rest of 1 Staffel of Kampfgeschwader 55 touched down at Villacoublay Airport, near Paris. The Airport had only been overrun by the advancing German forces the week before as they had entered Paris. Luftwaffe land crews had been busy preparing the airport for Gruppe's I, II, III and now their barracks, fuel depot and ammunition stores were all ready for Bernhard Schmitt and the other pilots and crew of his advance unit.

He was glad to be out of the tents they had been living in for the last few days. The smell had reminded him of camping trips with the school and the heat had been almost unbearable.

As the last of the engines were switched off, a relative silence descended over the base. Bernhard and Willie walked out after inspecting their new quarters to take a look at the new arrivals. Many hands were shaken as the crews descended from their planes and walked towards the tower, passing the two friends who were walking the other way.

'They seem so young,' he whispered to Willie, as another new pilot shook his hand on the way to his new home.

'They're the same age as us,' Willie replied. 'It's just that they haven't seen the things we have seen, that will age them soon enough, especially when they do battle with the damned RAF.'

Bernhard smiled at Willie. He was right, all of this fighting had made him feel old. He was sure his hair was starting to turn grey already.
'Let's hope they are as lucky as we have been Willie,' he added. 'Maybe we won't fight the RAF for long. Perhaps there will be a truce.'

'Fat chance of that my friend,' said Willie. 'As long as that Churchill is in charge, I can't see him shaking hands with Hitler any time soon.'

Bernhard tried to imagine Churchill and Hitler shaking hands and sharing a joke but he just couldn't picture it. Willie was right, this war wasn't over yet.

As they walked around, they were impressed with the new Heinkels and when they got a fair distance away from the tower they looked back and were amazed at just how much Villacoublay had changed in such a short time. The airport seemed enormous and the building seemed to offer them so much space that they could have accommodated many more Gruppes if needed. Building works were going on everywhere they looked. More accommodation was being built, bunkers were being dug out and gun emplacements were sprouting up everywhere.

Once again, he marveled at the prowess of the German war machine and how quickly the powers that be could get things done.

On the way back to the mess, he and Willie spoke about Paris. They had been promised the chance to visit the centre of Paris later in the week and they were all looking forward to seeing the Eiffel Tower and sampling French cuisine.

Over breakfast the excitement levels were high as news had spread that the French were going to sign an Armistice today and the war in Europe would effectively be over. Hitler had ordered that the meeting would be held in the same place that the 1918 German surrender had been signed. The dignitaries would gather in the very same railway carriage in the Forest of Compiegne where the last war ended for Germany and the seeds of this war were sown, thanks to the reparations requested by the allies at the Paris Peace Conference in 1919.

That carriage had been taken from a museum in Paris to the chosen site the day before. Bernhard had heard that some of the fighter pilots would be flying over the Forest of Compiegne to provide protective cover but also as a demonstration of force to the defeated French leaders.

Bernhard and Willie were also excited to find out from the Oberleutnant that one of the row of 9 sleek, new Heinkel 111 bombers sitting on the concrete was waiting for them. All were sporting the red griffin with black wings which formed K.G. 55's crest. It seems they had some new planes to play with as well as their new facilities. *The German war machine is truly amazing,* he thought as the two friends drank a last coffee before leaving the mess.

Also, joining them at Villacoublay were Aufklarungsgruppe 123 who were scheduled to move nearer the coast as soon as possible. Their Dornier 17E's and 17F's looked sleek and fast and they would prove good companions for the next week or so as the battle moved out of Europe and on to British shores. The British called the Dorniers, 'Flying Pencils'.

To cap it all General der Fleiger, Hugo Sperrle the Commander of Luftflotte 3 (Air Fleet 3) was due to visit their base soon. It was rumoured he wanted to see what progress had been made on the facilities at Villacoublay and to congratulate the pilots on the success of what had been the Battle of France. Who knows, someone had said, Hitler might come with him.

After breakfast, and a bit like excited school boys, they ran across to the new planes and after a quick word with the ground crew were soon crawling through the narrow confines of their new Heinkel 111, getting used to the new layout and seeing where improvements had been made. The most obvious change was the nose, which had been radically redesigned to give the pilot and navigator/bomb aimer a better view.

They sat in their respective seats for a while and discussed what to call their new Heinkel. After some debate, they decided on Lili. After Lili Marleen, a love song that he had heard a year or so ago but which the Nazi party had banned. If anyone asked they would say it was in memory of his grandmother, who was also called Lili.

As they sat there, Bernhard could not get used to the amazing change in the cockpit and the panoramic view he had through the all glass nose of the plane. It did give him a brief feeling of vulnerability but he was sure he would get used to it.

Bernhard sat in the left-hand pilot seat and Willie sat alongside him. Below him and to his right was his only blind spot. A platform was located there for the bomb aimer who would double as the nose gunner. During a fight the co-pilot would move back to man the dorsal gun while a gunner would man the belly gun and the waist guns would be operated by the navigator. That means they would be getting an extra crew member.

The old Heinkel 111s had been hopelessly out gunned in the initial stages of the Battle for France and these new versions they hoped would turn the tide back in their favour. The time to test the new planes would come soon.

Now the rest of 1 Staffel of Kampfgeschwader 55 were all at Villacoublay there was one last ritual to perform.

Bernhard and five of the original pilots that had established themselves at Villacoublay brought out a coffin and ceremoniously carried it across to a small pyre the ground crew had built for them over the last few days on the edge of the apron.

They placed the coffin on the pyre and all of the pilots and crew of Kampfgeschwader 55 gathered around. The coffin had the crest of the Staffel crudely drawn on the side as well as the words *"Zum Tod und Zum Sieg"*. To Death and to Victory.

Several bottles of schnapps were passed around and then the Oberleutnant gave the toast.

'To those that don't return and to victory.'

They all cheered and drank their schnapps.

What was left in the bottles was poured over the coffin and pyre. The Oberleutnant lit a match and threw it on to the pyre and the whole lot went up in flames.

They all cheered again.

The ritual was complete. Those crews that didn't come back had been given their funeral ceremony.

Now all they had to do was stay alive for the last push against Britain.

The group split up as they walked away from the dwindling fire. Bernhard was chatting with Willie and the two K's when a man came running across the airfield. He called to him and Willie to hurry to the briefing room. They had a new mission.

Within the hour, Bernhard was in the air, an extra crew member had been hurriedly found and his mission was to bomb an RAF base near Exeter on the South Coast of England. Kass had been welcomed aboard by Bernhard and the rest of the crew. The two K's had become the 3 K's and they all laughed at that. He seemed genuine and came with excellent credentials as a navigator and gunner. Willie would still take the bomb aimer role for now until Kai was properly trained up in that role. Willie was also an excellent gunner so could handle the nose gun. That gave them four gunners and Bernhard felt, as a crew, they were well prepared.

The day was bright and clear and it soon became hot in the 'greenhouse' as he had christened the cockpit of his new Heinkel. The crew were on full alert as the small group of 6 planes (two *Kette*'s) crossed the battered remains of Cherbourg.

From there they headed north of Alderney and then west down the Channel towards Exeter.

The coast of England was clearly laid out before them but before they reached land Willie spotted around 6 black dots high in the sky off their starboard side. Believing in strength in numbers, Bernhard gave the order to keep in tight formation and together they prepared for battle.

The hurricanes attacked in line astern and it soon became apparent that the Heinkel's extra fire power was still no match for the fast-moving fighters.

Within minutes, two of the Heinkels were pouring smoke from damaged engines and another was falling behind and banking off to port. 3 parachutes quickly blossomed, Bernhard wondered if the pilot and co-pilot had been killed.

Realising the futility of the raid and the suicidal nature of the battle, Bernhard ordered the remaining planes to break formation and head back to base as best they could. He also told them to jettison their bombs to try and make extra speed.

He spotted Schulz, his wingman, heading off with one of the Hurricane's in hot pursuit but he had little time to worry about him.

Bernhard pushed forward on the stick as soon as his bombs were gone and dived forward. Turning hard to port he hoped to be able to lose his attackers against the background of the sea. One hurricane spotted him and gave chase.

Bullets were soon flashing by and he felt the Heinkel take hits. All guns were blazing now trying to fight back but the Hurricane seemed to know all the best angles to attack from.

He dropped lower to push the Hurricane above him and was soon skimming the waves. He could see the Hurricanes bullets making trails in the water as he tried to avoid the cannon fire.

Then, as suddenly as the attack had begun, it was over. The fighter had seemingly run out of ammunition. A Hurricane only had enough ammunition to fire its guns for 15 seconds and so couldn't engage in combat for long.

He told the three K's to cease fire.

In one of those strange peaceful moments in war, the Hurricane pilot drew alongside Bernhard's Heinkel and with a wave and a waggle of his wings, he pulled up and headed away.

Breathing a heavy sigh of relief Bernhard gradually lifted his battered plane to 300 metres above sea level and plotted a course back to France. This time he flew low over the island of Herm, then on across Sark and north of Jersey on his route back to Paris. Fuel was beginning to run low so he eased back the throttles and gently eased his plane over the French coast and across the green fields of northern France. He looked at his watch, it wasn't even noon, yet it seemed like they had been flying and fighting for hours.

The Midlands, England

After getting little sleep, dawn had brought an early awakening for Rachel as she journeyed north through the Midlands of England. She had never heard of any of the places they were passing and her curiosity was now getting the better of her. Her eyes, reddened by hours of crying, now focused on the world outside of the train window. The rhythmic drumming of the train wheels became normal for her, just as it was for many frightened children on the train.

As she sat by the window she noticed odd things. Fields full of corn, black and white cows and no sea. In fact, she had never appreciated just how big the world really was. Huge hills would appear from time to time and then disappear again, forests appeared that seemed to go on forever and lakes, she had never seen a lake before.

She had completely lost track of time and wondered what her family were doing back in Guernsey. A bit of her started to wish they were all together so she could show them all these wonderful things she was seeing.

A field full of horses brought a smile to her face, particularly when one started to run towards the train as if it wanted a race.

Then more fields, this time full of sheep. She had never seen a sheep before so this was amazing. She was soon chatting with the other girls in the carriage and her teacher smiled thankfully that the trauma of the day before seemed to be over. As their curiosity mounted she too found herself engrossed in the world passing their window and talked with the girls about what they were seeing.

It was only 10 o'clock in the morning but Guernsey seemed a million miles away as the train took them ever further north.

St Peter Port, Guernsey

The office door opened, snapping him back to the present. He had been miles away, imagining Rachel's train being attacked by a German bomber, thankfully it was just a daydream – he was very tired. The secretary was back from her morning break and soon the typewriter was clicking away again and he had to get on with his work. At noon, he decided he needed to stretch his legs. His eyes were tired and his back was beginning to ache.

He walked towards the St Julian Emplacement and headed over to where a group of drivers were eating sandwiches. As he crossed the jetty, a roaring filled the air and a Heinkel bomber flew low over the harbour, pursued by a Hurricane fighter. A cheer went up from the drivers and the sound of machine guns rattled across the harbour as the planes headed south. A faint trail of smoke drifted down on to the harbour but he couldn't be sure which plane was hit.

The two protagonists disappeared beyond the high ground to the south of St Peter Port. As they vanished from sight, some spent shell casings from the Hurricane's guns fell in the road with a tinkling sound.

Life quickly got back to normal and Laurence crossed the road, picking up one of the shell cases as he made his way to the group of drivers for a quick chat. As they started talking the Hurricane reappeared from the south and did a victory roll over the Harbour before heading north to England, waggling his wings as he went. The chap next to him clapped Laurence on the back. 'That's one less Jerry to worry about eh!'

Laurence smiled back and absent mindedly looked north. The war was getting closer. Men and women were dying all around the islands. The people in France were conquered, England was relatively quiet for now but how long would it be before Hitler turned his full attention there. London was already prepared for air raids and all that stood between Germany and England was the Channel and the young pilots of the RAF. He knew that Guernsey couldn't avoid the suffering for much longer. Decisions had to be made and he had to think of his wife and children above all else.

He looked at the shell case still in his hand and wondered if this was the bullet that downed the German plane. He put the bullet in his pocket and with a wave to the drivers started to head back to the office.

Tony, one of the drivers that Laurence had been talking to shouted after him.

'Hey Laurence, does that missus of yours want a job?'

'Why, what's happening?' he said stopping and turning back to look at the driver.

'Bert Martel has a dozen greenhouses full of tomatoes and no one to pick 'em,' explained Tony. 'If she wants some work tell her to pop down the Braye Road to see Bert. He'll be the tired looking guy picking tomatoes on his own.'

Tony laughed and climbed back into his truck to get another load.

Laurence decided to discuss it with Lily over tea. The extra money would be good and it might take her mind off Rachel.

L.G. 55's New HQ, Villacoublay, Paris, France

Bernhard Schmitt had landed his bullet ridden Heinkel in a cloud of smoke and the crew had bailed out quickly in case it caught fire. They stood and applauded Bernhard for getting them back safe as he climbed out of the plane last. 'Lucky Dog,' Kai called out and they all laughed.

He then rushed straight into de-briefing. He told the Oberleutnant how they had been bounced by a squadron of Hurricanes just north of Alderney and the two *Kette's* of three Heinkel's each had broken in all directions. He had headed south and then east while he had spotted Schulz Barhoff, his wingman, heading further south with a Hurricane on his tail. Bernhard also told the Oberleutnant how he had been lucky as his pursuer had run out of ammunition. He explained how his last glimpse of Schulz had been to see him diving towards the sea and heading south with a fighter in hot pursuit, guns blazing.

Now he was worried and wanted to hear if there was any news of Schulz.

He faced an anxious wait. In fact, he waited for an hour until they received a report from a naval unit near St Malo that a Heinkel had been seen making a forced landing in the sea off the French coast. A fast patrol boat had rescued the pilot who had been wounded, but his Radio Operator and co-pilot had been killed by enemy gunfire. The two gunners were missing, presumed drowned.

With two other aircraft known to be missing, Bernhard could just pray that if this was Schulz, he was safe and not too badly injured. He made his way down to the mess and drank a schnapps to toast his friend and another to mourn the loss of the dead and missing crew.

Several more Heinkels from K.G. 55 had landed with damage and the ground crews were busy repairing the bullet holes, inspecting engines and where it was safe, refueling the planes ready for their next patrols. It seemed his hopes that things were going to get easier were hopelessly awry. The reality may well be that the nearer they got to England the tougher the opposition was going to be. Just a quick look at the row of Heinkels told the story. What this morning had been a row of 9 brand new aircraft had been reduced to 6, with three of those suffering various levels of damage.

With so much repair work to do he was grounded for the rest of the day. After a sleepy afternoon in his deckchair with Greif by his side, and a copy of Signal Magazine, he decided to take a walk around the airport perimeter as the sun dropped low in the west.

It was the longest day of the year and he loved these late summer evenings. He said a small prayer as he stood and watched the sunset, grateful for his safe return from the Exeter raid earlier in the day. He stopped by one of the anti-aircraft gun batteries and smoked an Eckstein cigarette with the gunners. They discussed the rumour that the invasion of England would start soon.

He decided he must write a letter home when he got back to the newly established barracks; he had to tell his family about this day. He turned his back on the sunset and headed to the mess, *time for one more drink*, he decided.

Meanwhile in the new Paris Luftwaffe HQ, orders had been received from Berlin to prepare an expeditionary force to invade Guernsey, the first piece of British soil to be occupied. A small force of crack German troops was being assembled and three Auntie Ju's (Junkers JU-52) troop transports had been assigned to the invasion. They were due to land in Villacoublay on Friday the 29th June.

The big news in the mess was that planning for the invasion of England was well underway. Operation Sealion, as it was code named, would start with the Luftwaffe gaining control of the air and plans were being put in place to destroy English airfields in the south east. Pilots in every Luftwaffe mess across France and Germany talked about nothing else.

The trouble was on today's evidence getting control of the air over the channel would be no easy task. The Hurricanes were fearsome fighters and he had heard that the Spitfires the British flew were better yet. Invading Britain might not be as easy as everyone seemed to think.

Crewe, Cheshire, England

The train full of Guernsey children finally pulled into Crewe Station after a long journey of almost 24 hours. The trip had included several stops and several diversions, but for the first time in a day, Rachel was able to stretch her legs in the open air. The girls stuck together as they took a short walk to a local school hall where they were given a proper meal and somewhere to sleep for the night. Rachel found three sweets in various pockets and corners of her bag and shared them with her two friends. They chose three camp beds together and were having a good chat, wondering where they were going. Suddenly a stern looking man with a black tin hat on his head burst into the room.

'Lights out!' He shouted. One girl screamed in shock.

'Lights out - NOW!' He shouted again.

The lights were turned off immediately.

As he shut the door the hall was plunged into darkness. Several of the children could be heard crying but in a while they all settled down.

Soon they were all asleep, worn out by the journey. Rachel dreamed of sunny beaches, her family and more than anything her mum. *Where was her mum? When would she see her again?* Had been her last thoughts before the dreams began.

Guernsey

How Laurence got through the rest of the day he would never know. Paperwork was completed, the boats sailed as normal and the skies remained clear and blue.

5.30pm finally came, he left the office, walking quickly to the shop to get the evening paper. He waited at the bus stop by the old parish pump, tucking the paper he had bought into his jacket pocket.

He felt the shell case in his pocket and pulled it out, turning it over and over in his hand thinking about how much damage such a small thing could do. He didn't even notice when the green number 10 bus pulled up.

It took a shout from the bus driver to break his train of thought. 'Are you coming mate?'

'Sorry,' he stuttered.

He took a seat by the window at the back of the bus and pondered the next few days. *What should they do?*

He slipped the shell case back into his pocket and then unfolded the paper. He eagerly read for news of the school party but found nothing. The paper was full of appeals for the island to get back to normal and for people to remain calm. It was reported that some farmers had killed their cattle before they had left the island. Times were hard for many and worse was to come.

But it was Friday and he had been paid. In his jacket pocket, he had his pay packet and he decided to squirrel as much of it away as he could, just in case.

Over tea Laurence mentioned to Lily the idea of her getting a job picking tomatoes. She agreed it would be a good idea but she needed to check with Ma that she would be happy to look after Laura and Michael.

'If she's happy I'll have a walk down to his vinery on Monday. Let's enjoy the weekend first eh!' she said in her soft Guernsey accent.
Tea was fish, it was always fish on a Friday. It was a local pollack Lily had been given by a neighbour. It was served with mash and cabbage and went down a treat. After tea, they all walked over to the seafront and took a stroll as far as the tram sheds and back to work off their meal.

On the way back, they had walked down to the beach and collected a bucket of shells which Michael would play with the following day.

Skimming stones had been the game of choice and Michael had managed two bounces and was justly proud of his achievement. He spoke of nothing else as they walked back.

Friday was also bath night and once they were back Lily started boiling kettles and lit a fire under the copper in their shed as Laurence filled it with water using a bucket. The tin bath was put in the shed and filled with the hot water as soon as each kettle boiled and soon the copper began to steam. The twins went first with Laura and Michael sharing the water. Carbolic soap was the order of the day and the smell permeated the house as it drifted in from the shed. Laurence followed as Lily dried the twins and put them to bed. Michael was still talking about skimming stones as Lily tucked him under the covers.

She was just about to leave him when in a sleepy voice, he asked. 'Where's Rachel?'

'She's on holiday in England,' Lily replied, tears welling up in her eyes. There was no response, Michael was away in the land of nod and no more awkward questions would be asked today.

Lily went back downstairs and put the kettle on to heat more water. She then washed Laurence's back as he relaxed in the bath. She brought him a dry towel and his dressing gown and then it was her time to get in the bath.

She topped the bath up with more hot water and then got her own soap out of the cupboard under the kitchen sink. No carbolic for Lily, and heaven forbid anyone else used her precious Dial soap.

Laurence admired her beautiful body as she climbed into the bath and helped wash her back and massaged her head using the soap as a shampoo. He boiled the kettle again but stopped before it got too hot and then after testing the temperature rinsed her hair with the water straight from the kettle.

After a few minutes relaxing in the warm water, he brought her towels and soon she too was dry and cosy, hair wrapped in a small towel and wearing her big fluffy dressing gown which came down to her ankles.

Laurence started tipping the water down the drain using the bucket until the bath was light enough to carry. Then together they carried the bath to the back door and Laurence tipped the bath up and emptied the rest of the water directly into the outside drain.

Lily had the kettle back on and soon they were snuggled on the settee with a cup of tea.

Instead of the radio, Laurence put on one of his precious 33 rpm records and they sat enjoying the music. He picked up the paper and Lily got out her knitting. She was working on a cardigan for Rachel, although she didn't know when she would give it to her.

Laurence suddenly remembered the shell casing and went to his jacket and took out the shell case and handed it to Lily.

'Where did you get this?' She asked.

He explained about the Hurricane chasing the German Bomber and how the shell casings had fallen from the sky.

As she turned it over in her hand they talked about how that shell case had made its journey from an arms factory in England to their front room. She got up and placed it on the mantelpiece next to her father's photograph. It seemed a fitting place for it.

They headed off to bed at around 10.30pm, and for a while Lily lay awake, thinking of her precious Rachel and wondering what had happened to her.

For once, Laurence had fallen straight to sleep and feeling safe in Laurence's arms and lulled by his gentle breathing, she eventually succumbed to her exhaustion and fell into a troubled sleep.

Villacoublay, Paris, France

Bernhard had made sure the blackout curtain was fixed in place and then took out a small leather case which contained his diary, writing paper and envelopes. They had been a present from his parents and went everywhere with him. A pen and ink set sat on the small desk in his room, pilot's perks, and by the light of a candle he put pen to paper.

Dear Mutter and Vater

I miss you so much. Today has been a difficult day, one of my best friends was nearly killed. I know now that he is safe but he has lost some of his crew and has been injured so I am unlikely to see him again for some time.

We have settled down here in France and I am looking forward to sometime in Paris, to see the sights. I hope all is well at home and life is being good to you. Tell Greta I love her and miss her too.

I am looking forward to some leave and the chance to come home and enjoy Mutter's cooking. I miss your home baked bread most of all.

They have given me a new plane to fly which looks and feels great. I hope I am making you proud. One day after the war is over, I hope I can take you all for a flight so you can see and feel what it is like to fly in these magnificent machines.

Well I must get some rest now. Give the Wolf a pat and a bone from me and hopefully I will see you soon.

Love to you both.

Your Son

Bernhard x

It was a hot night. Bernhard stripped down to his shorts and climbed into his cot and snuggled down under the single sheet. He blew out the candle. The smell of the smoke reminded him of home and he drifted off into a deep, trouble free sleep, dreaming of log fires, running through the woods with Greta and the Wolf and swimming in the river Elbe.

Chapter 4 – Saturday 22nd June 1940

In the News

France signs armistice with Germany
French blow up the port of La Rochelle to avoid it falling into German hands
Vichy France is created while the northern half of the country and all the West Coast is occupied by German forces

St Peter Port, Guernsey

With tomato production reaching its peak there was no rest for Laurence, despite it being a Saturday. After a couple of slices of toast, layered with rich yellow Guernsey butter, he was off again to work.

It was just 7am.

His boss had promised him that he would be finished by noon and he was looking forward to spending some time with Lily and the children that afternoon. The paper was out early today and the news was all about an emergency committee being formed to manage the island in the current circumstances.

Ways to run the farms and greenhouses, abandoned by those that had left, had to be found. Some businesses were advertising 'business as usual' despite losing some of their workers. He was amazed that it was estimated some 13,000 people had already left the island. Most interesting to Laurence though was an article which stated that tickets were not required for any women, children or men of military age wishing to be evacuated.

He now knew that if things got serious he could ensure Lily, Laura and Michael were safe by getting them off the island at any time.

The work was constant as the trail of lorries being unloaded grew by the hour but at noon, as promised, his boss took over the afternoon shift which gave Laurence the chance to get away. He ran down the quay and just caught the bus at ten minutes past twelve and was soon back home.

As it was a beautiful day they decided to take a picnic up to Delancey Park and enjoy the views across to the harbour of St Peter Port.

They filled a picnic basket and left the house, locking up before heading off. They walked along the front and then up Delancey Lane and cut through into the park behind the school house. The Sausmarez Tower stood tall in the afternoon sun and seemed like it had always been there and would last forever.

They sat next to the tower and enjoyed a feast of freshly picked crab that had been cooked that morning in the copper in their shed. Cheese, homemade bread, Guernsey gauche with Guernsey butter and lemonade.

Ma had joined them on the park and brought with her some cakes and Guernsey sweets and together they enjoyed a wonderful, family, afternoon. Michael and Laura played on the swings and they even had time for a bit of football, which Michael enjoyed the most. He was virtually attached to that battered old football of his.

Laurence had made a kite out of old papers and for a while they ran around trying to get it to fly. At first there hadn't been enough wind but after lunch they tried again and soon it was soaring above the park and they all took turns to hold the string.

This brought a huge smile to Laura's face as she had been responsible for adding brightly coloured ribbons to the kite's tail and was enthralled to see their creation sailing high in the sky.

For once the war seemed a million miles away and perhaps life could get back to some semblance of normality.

They made plans for Sunday and toasted Rachel with the lemonade, hoping she was safe and well wherever she was. It went quiet for a while after that, Laurence dozing in the sun with his handkerchief on his head. Lily lay with her head on his chest and closed her eyes, deep in thought. Michael wasn't one to respect silence for long and soon he was running around like a mad thing, chasing Laura about and kicking his ball against the base of the tower. He finished off trying to climb the tower but then fell and cut his knee which ended with Lily nursing him and tying Laurence's handkerchief around the graze.

Michael was soon off again, kicking the ball and seemingly proud of his 'bandage'.

Crewe, Cheshire, England

Rachel woke to the smell of cooking, crying children and a babel of noise. For a moment, she couldn't remember where she was. This was the first morning after a good night's sleep that she hadn't woken up in her precious bed back in Guernsey.

They sat down in a big hall to a breakfast of porridge with some toast and jam. Rachel had never eaten porridge before but she found it quite nice. Christine and Julie sat with her and then by rota they were off to the bathrooms to get themselves ready for the day. Some boys ran around the hall chasing each other, playing at airplanes dogfighting as they frequently did in the skies above them.

In no time, they were packing their small cases again and walking back towards the train station. As a railway town, she felt the place looked a bit dark and grimy, the cloudy day didn't help. She also noticed signs for the Rolls Royce factory and wondered what a factory was. She was also amazed to see gun emplacements, manned by men in khaki uniforms and protected by walls of sandbags and above them floated huge barrage balloons, the first she had seen. Tears filled her eyes again as she thought of home and her family, and she longed to see the sea and smell fresh, salty air.

Within a few minutes, they were back on the train, and this time feeling much less stressed, she spotted the engine smoking away at the head of the train and the guards on the platform in their uniforms. For a Guernsey girl this was all incredible, if not magical. She had never experienced anything quite like this.

Soon after a lot of whistling the train jerked forward and they were off again to more pastures new.

Villacoublay, Paris, France

Bernhard watched as the ground crew once again worked on his aircraft. His new Heinkel was now covered with a mass of patches, each marking where a Hurricane bullet had passed through the metal skin of the fuselage and wings. As he sat in his deckchair in the sun with his new found canine friend asleep at his feet, he noticed two crews leave their barracks and head towards the Dornier 17s of Aufklarungsgruppe 123.

Before long the two aircraft were taking to the air and heading west towards the Brittany coast. He wondered where they might be off to and called over one of the ground crew who was heading back towards the barracks after seeing their aircraft off the ground.

After a quick conversation, he learned that they were off to carry out a reconnaissance mission over the Channel Islands. He frowned as he thought what the reason for such a mission might be but soon put those thoughts aside as a ripple of excitement suddenly gripped the men around him.

The rumours had been correct. The General der Fleiger was due to visit Villacoublay at noon. He had to polish his boots and make sure his dress uniform was fit for duty. The parade of all air crew and ground staff had been called for 11.45am.

For a moment, he envied the Dornier crews that had just taken off, *at least they don't have to polish their shoes,* he thought as he scampered back to his billet.

But at least he wouldn't be flying into any danger today.

Delancey Park, Guernsey

Laurence was taking a walk around the park, arm in arm with Lily, as the children played under the watchful eye of Ma. As they walked they discussed Rachel and how she might be getting on in England. They still had no idea where she had gone.

There were many people strolling in the park but there was a notable shortage of school age children in the play area compared to normal weekends. It was a stark reminder of what was happening in the island.

Other couples were having a turn around the park when the droning sound of an airplane invaded the peace and quiet. Couples and families all around the park were stopping and looking for the source of the sound. Laurence eventually spotted the speck high in the sky. He pointed to the speck and others around them followed his lead. It was impossible to tell what type of plane it was or who's side it was on but as they watched it began circling around obviously looking down on what was happening below.

Eventually the plane moved off to the south and everyone got back to enjoying the day. Laurence and Lily were walking around the south east corner of the park when they noticed people pointing off towards St Peter Port. From their vantage point they could see the road to St Peter Port and the lines of tomato trucks still queuing to unload. It was only at the last minute that they noticed what the fuss was all about.

A German Dornier "flying pencil" was heading almost straight at them, coming in at roof top height and angling up to fly over the park at less than 100 feet. It had come from the direction of St Peter Port.

It suddenly became obvious that it wasn't on its own.

They could see a plane behind it and then heard the sharp chatter of machine gun fire. It was being pursued by a Bristol Blenheim, fighter bomber.

The Blenheim was firing the occasional burst from its wing mounted machine gun but was being careful not to endanger the people in the park. Nevertheless, the families began to scatter in all directions, dropping to the ground if they were in the open, as the hunted and the hunter flashed overhead.

Just a few of the younger children stared fascinated at the planes, oblivious to the danger and watching intently as they flew over their heads and disappeared off to the north.

People began to pick themselves up, brushing off grass cuttings and straightening their clothes.

Laurence helped Lily to her feet, and for a moment, they held each other tight. Shouts of 'Dadda, Dadda,' brought them back to reality and young Michael came running over to them.

'Did you see them Dadda? The planes, the planes.'

Laurence scooped the excited Michael up into his arms and hugged him tight.

'I saw them son. I saw them!'

They walked over to Ma who was cuddling Laura. Laura was in floods of tears, obviously terrified by seeing the planes pass so close. Lily took over the cuddling and after Ma had packed up the picnic they headed home together, hand in hand. The incident had brought the war home to them again and the mood was more sombre on the way home.

Villacoublay, Paris, France

Bernhard was standing to attention in front of his plane as were all of the other crews based at Villacoublay. General der Fleiger, Hugo Sperrle was taking the salute as he was driven along in front of them.

It was 12 noon sharp.

Bernhard had to admit the parade was quite impressive and he felt a warm sense of pride as he stood there with his crew and the rest of his Gruppe. Eventually the black, open top car, flying two swastikas on the front wings turned and drew up in front of the assembled airmen and ground crew. The General der Fleiger had a word with the Generalmajor of Kampfgeschwader 55 and they were ordered to break ranks and gather around the car. Everyone rushed forward until the car was surrounded by smiling servicemen.

Hugo Sperrle stood tall and addressed the crowd.

'Congratulations my fine boys. You have made me very proud. Adolf Hitler, our glorious leader, sends his congratulations, through me, to all of you, on completing the victory we have here today. The Battle for France and for Europe has been won. Nothing stands in our way on the Continent, we are the victors and to us come the spoils. Enjoy France, enjoy your victory. But the war is not yet won. Next, we will invade Britain and then the war will be over. We will lead the way to the final victory, we my boys will destroy the Royal Air Force and leave the door open for the Wehrmacht to walk ashore in victory.' There was a huge roar and cheers of 'Sieg Heil, Seig Heil, Seig Heil.'

With the cheers echoing around the aerodrome, Hugo Sperrle was driven away.

As the parade dispersed, the Dorniers returned. One was trailing a faint ribbon of smoke and Bernhard noticed one propeller wasn't spinning. More importantly the wheel on the side of the plane with the damaged engine wasn't fully down as it made its approach.

Suddenly the shrill noise of sirens split the air and a fire tender and ambulance were racing out towards the runway. He had been walking back towards the mess but when he saw the plane in trouble he turned and started to run out towards the runway, just as the Dornier touched down on its one good wheel.

For a while the pilot managed to keep the plane level but as he lost speed, the right-hand wing dipped and the broken propeller touched the runway. What happened next seemed like slow motion to Bernhard.

As the plane lost more speed a shower of sparks poured from the right-hand wing tip and the plane started to spin to the right. As he watched, the left-hand wing seemed to give the plane some lift and slowly but surely the plane flipped on to its back.

He could see the pilot fighting the controls, and then let go, as he realised he could do no more. He clasped his head in his hands as if to brace himself against the impending crash. For a brief second their eyes met across the 100 or so metres between them, and then with a sickening crash and the scream of tearing metal, the plane landed on its back.

Bernhard knew the pilot would not survive such a crash. The explosion which followed would put pay to any lingering hope for the rest of the crew. Bernhard was thrown to the ground as the shock wave blew over him. It seemed to him that the plane must have had at least one bomb on board or a pretty full fuel tank.

The ambulance that had been nearest the plane was blown over on its side but the fire tender was still on its wheels and soon they were working to get the fire under control.

Bernhard ran over to the ambulance and helped the crew out of the vehicle. Despite a few cuts and bruises they all seemed OK. Soon other vehicles were rushing to the scene to help clear the wreckage. The other Dornier was still circling over the airport waiting for clearance to land.

Bernhard traipsed back to his deckchair, Greif, the black Labrador was waiting for him. He stroked the dogs head as in his own head he relived what he had just witnessed. For some reason, his own mortality had not even crossed his mind until now, but that could have been him. The way his eyes had connected with that other pilot seconds before he died was an image he just couldn't shift. How quickly life can end, how vulnerable they all were.

I wonder if the General der Fleiger saw that, he thought. *The destruction of the RAF won't be as easy as Hugo Sperrle thinks.* He concluded to himself.

He sat back down in his deckchair and cried a silent tear for his unknown comrade. A man whose last contact with a human being had been eye contact with him. As his mind took it all in, he softly stroked the dog's head until satisfied, the dog flopped down and fell into a deep sleep.

As he sat he felt a trickle of liquid on the side of his head and thought he must be sweating in the summer heat but when he put his right hand to his head, his fingers came back red with blood. He realized, he must have been nicked by some flying debris from the plane as it exploded. Absently he licked the blood from his fingers and got up to walk back to the restrooms to wipe the blood from his face.

As he walked he decided he would find out the pilot's name and write about him in his diary.

Before he reached his billet, and still in his dress uniform, the second Dornier touched down. He couldn't believe how efficiently they had cleared the runway. The crew quickly exited the plane and headed over to the de-briefing room. One of the crew carried a box which Bernhard took to be a camera. No doubt some crucial information about the Channel Islands for the war effort he thought. Once again, he hoped the powers that be would leave the islands alone.

He turned and entered the building to find a wet cloth to clean his small wound. Bernhard suddenly realised it was the first injury he had received since the war had begun.

He really was lucky, he thought.

If that fragment had been a couple of inches to his left he wouldn't be walking back to clean himself up right now. He could be lying next that poor pilot under a blanket. The thought made him shiver, despite the heat of the day.

Glasgow, Scotland

After what had turned into quite an adventure, the train carrying Rachel and her school friends from Crewe, had crossed the Scottish border, and eventually pulled up in Queen's Park Station, Glasgow. She had been glued to the window all the way north as they passed through some of the most beautiful countryside she had ever seen. She had even caught a glimpse of Hadrian's Wall as they had entered Scotland, her teacher telling the girls all about its origins. Coming from such a small island, rolling hills and valleys were so completely new, she had been amazed at almost every turn of the wheels as the train wound its way into the heart of Scotland.

Once they reached Queen's Park they were all herded off the train into a large hall, a short walk from the platform. There they were all lined up and a crowd of people came in to meet them. Rachel, Christine and Julie held hands as people started to pick children and take them away.

They hadn't been able to hear above all the noise as a teacher had told them they were being assigned homes to stay in until the schools were reorganised, so this parade came as a bit of a shock.

Eventually a very smart couple came up to them and picked Rachel and Christine to go with them. Julie held on tight to Rachel's hand and bravely Rachel stood her ground.

'Can Julie come too Miss,' she asked bravely. 'We three are best friends.' A tear formed in her eyes and her bottom lip began to tremble.

The three girls held each other close until their fate was decided.

There was a brief discussion between the two adults and after a moment of hesitation the lady nodded her head and the three girls were told by one of their teachers to follow Her Ladyship. Still together and hand in hand they followed the grand couple out of the hall.

Outside the hall, a large black car was waiting for them and a man in a green, velvet looking, uniform opened the door for them. He smiled as they all looked on in wonder at the beautiful red leather interior of the Rolls Royce. The grand lady ushered them into the back of the car and the gentleman, after kissing the lady on the cheek, got in and sat in the front, next to the driver. The lady smiled at them, closed the car door and without a word walked back into the station. As the sun started to set, the car set off and they headed through the streets of Glasgow and then out into the Scottish countryside.

After an hour's drive, and in the failing light, they pulled off the road and headed down a long drive. They could see lights ahead as the car pulled up in front of the biggest house Rachel had ever seen.

People came out and took their tiny bags into the house and others spoke hurriedly with the gentleman, nodding and being very deferential. A large lady with an apron and a white hat came to the car and told them to follow her.

They duly went through the large front doors and were taken downstairs to a large kitchen where a feast was quickly prepared for them. Hot soup, warm bread and lots of milk were soon being consumed. The girls had forgotten just how hungry they were.

The large lady explained that she was Cook and tomorrow morning they would meet their 'Nanny' who would look after them while they stayed in the big house. A huge fire roared in the grate even though it was the middle of the summer and being full of food and nice and toasty the three girls started to feel sleepy.

Seeing them starting to struggle to keep awake, Cook took them back upstairs and showed them to their room, which was on the floor above the entrance hall level.

There were three beds in the room and each had a beautiful doll sitting on the pillow. Underneath each pillow was a set of warm pyjamas.

Rachel took the middle bed and was soon dressed in her pyjamas and tucked up under the covers. She cuddled her new doll and fell fast asleep.

St Sampsons, Guernsey

The family had headed home after their fright on the park. No-one had said much apart from Michael who was excited about seeing the planes so close. He had never seen anything like that before and as they walked home he was running around the family group, arms outstretched, making engine and machine gun noises and pretending to shoot down imaginary enemies.

He now wanted to be a pilot, he told his Dad, and fight the Germans. Lily wasn't too impressed, she loathed all fighting and as soon as they had finished their tea of leftovers from the picnic, Michael was packed off to his room to get ready for an early bed.

That evening after Laura had gone to bed and peace had been restored to the house Lily and Laurence sat for a while, as they always did, talking about the day and what had happened.

The radio played quietly in the background tuned in as usual to the Home Service. The enjoyment of the picnic was overwhelmed by the sudden closeness of the war. Both wondered what the outcome of the aerial chase had been and Lily hoped all involved had got back home safely. As she pointed out, all the men in the air, so close above them, were potentially, husbands, fathers or sons of someone who loved them and she couldn't bear the thought that lives may have been lost.

Laurence was more pragmatic, having been closer to violence than Lily. He knew that there had probably been a victor and a loser in that fight and it was unlikely both planes had got home safely. While outwardly agreeing with Lily in hoping that no-one got hurt, he secretly hoped the Blenheim had got home safely and the Dornier had been shot down.

Soon after 10pm, with Lily's eyes starting to close as she snuggled in to Laurence on their sofa, he gently touched her cheek. "Time for bed my love," he whispered and after he had turned off the radio, hand in hand they climbed the stairs to bed.

Villacoublay, Paris, France

Bernhard had made some enquiries and had found out the Dornier pilot's name. Heinz Klausman had been only 20 years old and had not long got his wings. He and his three-man crew had all died instantly as the Dornier 17F exploded on the runway. He was the pilot of one of two reconnaissance models in the Dornier Gruppe, it had been a sad loss to all who knew him. He had been known as the baby-faced pilot at Villacoublay, and many had either cast a fatherly eye his way, or ribbed him terribly about his looks.

He documented all of his brief memories and a few anecdotes he had picked up about the lad in his diary and wrote of his sadness in a letter home to his parents. However, as he finished the letter he thought of the effect it would have on his mother reading about the death, and the fear it might instill in her. Not wanting to scare her or upset her in any way he re-read the letter then tore it up and threw it in the wicker bin by his bed.

He picked up his copy of 'People without Space' by Hans Grimm and read for half an hour. He had to agree with the author that the Germans must be the most industrious race in the world. He could see the evidence all around him.

He blew out the candle next to his bed and knew he faced a restless night with dreams of Heinz staring at him in the last moments of his life.

He wasn't wrong.

Chapter 5 – Sunday 23rd June 1940

In the News

Adolf Hitler visits the Tourist sites in Paris
French and Italians start peace talks

Magloch House, 50 miles north of Glasgow, Scotland

After the best night's sleep for several days, Rachel awoke in their new home. They had been so tired the night before that they hadn't really taken in what their surroundings were like. They were each in single beds which were lined up in a row, with large windows in between each bed. The ceilings were incredibly high and a large chandelier hung from an elegant medallion in the middle of the room.

A large painting of a man and his dog against a hillside was on the wall above the fireplace, which was opposite the foot of the middle bed. Their small cases had been placed on top of three identical cupboards which were dotted around the walls. There was a large mirror which covered almost the whole of one wall which made the room seem even bigger. Several nice ornaments and candle sticks adorned the large mantelpiece above the fire.

Rachel was in the middle bed, and sat staring at her new surroundings, as the others stirred either side of her.

'Christine, Julie, wake up,' she whispered. 'We are in a palace!'

The other girls were soon sitting up and taking it all in. All three came from small homes and Rachel was convinced this room was bigger than her house back in Guernsey.

Soon they were up and about and excitedly looking out of the windows. The world seemed to go on for miles and miles, as the rolling Scottish hills and mountains glowed in the early morning sun. She could see cattle with huge horns in one field and sheep seemed to be dotted over every hillside. She could also see horses in a paddock, and what looked like a stable block, not far from the house. There were a few people at work already, feeding the horses and working on the gardens. The gardens were huge too, with fountains and flowers in abundance. It really was a fairy tale house, way beyond anything they could have imagined.

Rachel told the girls about a story her Mum had read to her of a princess in a beautiful castle – she was convinced that this was the very same castle and they would soon be meeting that princess.

At almost the very moment she mentioned the princess, there was a knock on the door.

'Come in,' Rachel called out and in came the most beautiful girl Rachel had ever seen. She was wearing a lovely blue, knee length dress and had black hair that framed a fresh, freckled face that seemed to shine as she beamed the biggest smile you could ever imagine.

'Hello lassies,' she said in a mild Scottish accent that had the girls looking at, and giggling to each other. 'My name is Mary and I am going to be your Nanny while you stay here in Magloch House.'

She asked them their names and where they were all from – she had never heard of Guernsey – and they chatted about their journey for a few minutes.

'Now who wants breakfast?' the Nanny asked.

The girls all put their hands up.

'OK girls, let's get you dressed and you can come down and see what Cook has made for you.'

She showed them that in each of the drawers were sets of clothes for them to wear. If anything was the wrong size or if they needed anything extra, all they had to do was ask.

The girls were stunned.

The clothes were so beautiful, they were like nothing they had ever seen before. They didn't know what to wear.

Mary saw their confusion. 'I am going to take you on a tour of the Estate so I suggest you wear dungarees, thick socks and a jumper. It may be summer but you could well find it chilly on the hills. There will be some boots ready for you downstairs so wear some slippers for now.'

'If you want a wash before you get dressed, you have your own bathroom across the hall and all the toiletries you will need are there waiting for you,' she continued. 'I'll give you ten minutes and then I'll come and get you.' Mary left them to it.

The girls were amazed. The house, the clothes, their own bathroom. Rachel was used to an outside toilet and a tin bath for a weekly wash.

In the bathroom, they found a tap with hot water, beautiful smelling soaps and brand new toothbrushes. Not a bar of carbolic soap was in sight. They really were in heaven.

Mary was soon back knocking on the door, and once she had checked that they were all properly dressed, she led them down to the kitchen. As they walked along the landing, they could see down into a large hall, which had a huge table with around 20 seats. The walls were all wooden and covered in stag's heads, paintings and several types of old fashioned weapons. There was even a suit of armour in one corner.

They went down some back stairs and were soon in the lower level of the house, which Mary told them was for the servants. They walked along a corridor with a stone floor, acutely aware of the glorious smells coming from Cook's kitchen. They were literally following their noses.

Mary told them the servants had all eaten at around 6am so they were the second shift. Rachel wasn't sure what that meant but was happy they were almost on their own in the huge kitchen. They sat at a large table and cook presented them with fried eggs, sausages, fried tomatoes and mushrooms and large lumps of brown bread. Mugs of steaming hot tea were also on the table as was milk if they wanted it.

They weren't going to starve!

Mary and Cook, whose real name was Pauline, although she preferred Cook, sat with them and chatted about their plans for the day. All three girls were particularly excited about seeing the horses and Mary told them that while they were here they would be taught how to ride. Both Cook and Mary just loved the way the girls ate, talked and smiled. 'Milady made a good choice', Rachel heard Cook whisper to Mary.

After breakfast Mary led the girls down to a rear entrance to the house, and in a boot room they found some wellington boots that were a perfect fit for them. Mary asked them to wait there for a moment while she got changed. Soon she was back in a set of blue overalls with a scarf tied in her hair and a lovely pink cardigan around her shoulders – Rachel thought she looked lovely. She too put boots on, and together they walked out into the morning sunshine. What was waiting for them was a complete shock.

A huge black horse stood in front of an open carriage. The carriage had two wheels and was highly polished. Mary told them it was a country cart. Mary helped Christine and Julie climb on to the seats which were looking back and she helped Rachel climb up into the seat next to her. Mary would be driving.

Mary told the girls the horse was called Jock and promised to give them all the chance to drive before the day was out. Cook came running out with a big wicker basket which she told them held a picnic and Christine and Julie were given the job of looking after it until lunch time.

Mary picked up the reins and with a flick and the words 'Walk on', Jock was on his way out of the back yard and walking them down towards the stables.

Guernsey

Sunday dawned clear and beautiful. Lily and Laurence decided to make the most of the day and visit the beach. Some routines should never change though and at 9.30am on the dot, Ma came to collect Laura and Michael and take them to Sunday school. They would all meet at Ma's house for Sunday dinner later.

Laurence and Lily went back into the house after they had waved them off and quickly made their way back to bed. Sunday morning was their time, the only time they were ever alone in the house.

After they had made love, they lay in each other's arms for a while before Lily turned over to gaze out of the window, deep in thought. Laurence gently rubbed her back, enjoying the feel of her skin.

'I love you so much,' Laurence whispered in her ear.

'I love you too.' Lily replied quietly.

'Wish we had more time like this.' Laurence added.

'No chance of that my love.' Lily replied laughing. 'Not in this house.'

'Maybe when the war is over, and after the children leave home. That will be our time.' Lily added.

'Can't wait.' Laurence whispered. Kissing her gently on the back of her neck.

They lay like that for a few minutes but time wasn't on their side, so they got dressed before gathering a few things to take to the beach. They decided not to go far and opted to take Ma and the children to Bordeaux, an area to the north of St Sampsons harbour, to sit on the beach below the Vale Castle.

They walked around to Ma, picnic basket in hand, just in time to see Ma and the children going inside Ma's house after Sunday school.

Lily turned her hand to helping Ma cook the usual Sunday roast and they all said grace before tucking in to an excellent spread of chicken and roast potatoes, with the families favourite - Yorkshire puddings.

After lunch, which ended with homemade rice pudding, and the dishes were done, the family enjoyed the 20-minute walk around to Bordeaux.

The tide was high so they sat on a blanket near the top of the beach. The adults enjoyed a paddle while the children went in for a dip.

Laurence kept a close eye on them to make sure they didn't get into any trouble.

Michael was hilarious in his new knitted bathers. As soon as he was wet they hung down almost to his knees making everyone howl with laughter.

Lily thought this was the first time she had heard them all laugh since Rachel left. As they sat and watched the children play they couldn't help but notice the steady flow of shipping between Guernsey and Herm, as the boatloads of freight and passengers left the harbour and headed towards England.

Later in the afternoon the food was unpacked from the picnic basket and laid out on the blanket. There was still crab left over from the day before and plenty of tomatoes and French bread, covered in Guernsey butter. Ma had brought along some wonderful smoked ham and cheese so a real feast was enjoyed by all.

At one point three planes had appeared overhead and they had thought there would be an attack on one of the boats but they turned out to be Bristol Blenhiems on a coastal patrol.

The sight raised a cheer from all of the families on the beach. Their presence was very reassuring, particularly when they turned and gave everyone a brief display, flying past in formation just a few hundred feet above their heads.

All too soon they had to head home, the sun was starting to get low in the west and Laurence and Lily wanted to get the children bathed before bed. Boiling the water in the copper would take a while.

They all walked home together. Ma would help bath the children before she went back to her house and normally Laurence would listen to the radio and perhaps read a few sheets of music. Keeping well out of the way.

Routine was so precious, particularly for the children.

When the time was right, Lily asked her mother if she would look after the children so she could go and work in the greenhouses, picking tomatoes. Ma was more than happy, as she loved the company, so it was agreed she would take them home with her tomorrow which would give Lily the chance to walk down the Braye Road to meet Bert Martel and see what the job involved.

While Lily put the children to bed, Laurence spent some time working on his bike in the back yard. He had noticed he had a slow puncture and with the help of a bucket of water and a puncture repair kit he managed to find the offending hole and repair it before it got too dark.

After settling down with a cup of Horlicks, and listening to the radio for an hour or so, they too went off to bed for a well-earned rest before work began in earnest for another week.

For once they slept well. It had been a good day and life seemed to be getting back to normal.

Villacoublay, Paris, France

Bernhard had enjoyed a good day too, but he knew his plane would be waiting for him in the morning and the briefing session he was going to that evening would set out their targets for the week.

That morning, along with Willie and several other crews, he had hitched a lift into Paris to do some sightseeing. The amazing news hit them as soon as they reached the city. France had surrendered, the war in France was over. Despite the surrender, he was amazed at just how busy the place was, and how life seemed to be going on as normal. German uniforms were everywhere but amongst them were the citizens of Paris going about their daily pursuits. People were strolling along the Champs Elysees, sitting outside of the hundreds of cafes, enjoying coffee and croissants, or just cycling along, enjoying the summer weather.

There was little interaction between the French people and the German troops apart from the waiters in the restaurants taking orders and the odd sly glance between some of the troops and groups of young French girls. Even Bernhard noticed he was receiving the odd admiring glance as he walked along the Boulevards of Paris in his smart dress uniform.

There were few signs of the war and a handful of the restaurants were even advertising their menus in German. *Life goes on I guess*, he thought.

During the afternoon, they found a cinema which was open and Bernhard decided to join the queue to watch Henri Decoin's latest film "Battement de Coeur". The others opted to sample several bottles of French wine, but Bernhard didn't drink that much, he liked a schnapps but only the occasional one, unless he was very stressed. The others left him with a few guarded taunts about his parentage but that didn't bother him, he was never that comfortable in a crowd, preferring his own company most of the time.

He knew a little French so was happy to sit and watch the film, enjoying the cool air of the theatre, rather than the heat of a Parisian afternoon. There were a few whispers around him as he took his seat but he wasn't worried at all as he felt no aggression from his fellow film goers.

During the interval, he queued with the others for an ice-cream and was polite as he let a couple of elderly French women go in front of him in the queue. He felt more like a tourist than a conquering hero.

As he walked back to his seat, one elderly Frenchman spat on the carpet in front of him, as he walked up the aisle, but he ignored it and the muttered curse that went with it. He just calmly took his seat and watched as the man's wife cuffed the old boy around the ear and told him to be careful.

Before the second half of the film started there was a note displayed on the screen informing everyone that a night time curfew had been introduced and requiring shutters and blackout curtains to be put in place as soon as it was dark. The note was by order of the commandant of the occupying forces. A few isolated groans and boos accompanied the notice but they were quickly silenced when the lights went down and the film restarted.

He laughed and almost cried as the romantic comedy unfolded and admired the beauty of the star, Danielle Darrieux. He was almost sorry the film had to end, as the reality of war was outside in that sunny Parisian afternoon.

He stayed in his seat as everyone left and a pretty young French girl stopped to ask if he was all right. In his faltering French, he replied that he was fine and she left him alone with his thoughts. He was thinking of home.

Eventually he stood up and made his way back out into the busy Paris street and headed off towards the Arc de Triomphe, where they had all agreed to meet, and where the truck would collect them and take them back to Villacoublay.

Suddenly there was a huge commotion ahead and a sizeable crowd had gathered. He managed to get a good vantage point and there, driving past, was a military cortege of black cars, each flying the Swastika. The centre car had soldiers riding on the running boards and sitting in the front seat, next to the driver, was Hitler himself.

He seemed to look straight at Bernhard as he drove by, heading towards the Arc de Triomphe, waving to the crowds. Bernhard saw some Parisians in tears, particularly a few of the older men. There were a few jeers from the crowds but enough

German servicemen were around to ensure Hitler saw many friendly faces.

During his sightseeing visit, Hitler would take a trip up the Eiffel Tower, enjoy the opera and take in Napoleon's tomb. Albert Speer, Hitler's Architect, accompanied him on the visit, perhaps thinking how the architecture of the new Europe would look in the future.

As Bernhard and his friends drove back to Villacoublay, the driver was given a few packets of cigarettes in return for a small diversion to the Palace of Versailles. A few of the airmen had cameras and the group had their photos taken in front of Versailles, these would be added to the images of him in front of the Eiffel Tower and the Arc de Triomphe taken earlier in the day and sent home to his parents.

It was a remarkable day and Bernhard could hardly believe he had seen Hitler himself in Paris and witnessed the Swastikas flying in these prominent, well known places, where the French tricolour had been flying just a few days before. Once again, he marvelled at the power of the German war machine. His belief in their ultimate success in whatever lay before them was renewed.

He couldn't wait for their next mission.

When they got back to base the first thing he noticed was that the Messerschmitts of Jagdgeschwader 26 had gone. Full of questions they sat down for the evening briefing. First came confirmation of the surrender of France, that was followed by the news that plans were being prepared to invade Britain, if needed.

The Oberleutnant was hopeful that Britain would surrender before the drastic step of crossing the channel had to be taken, particularly as the British forces were in chaos after the evacuation at Dunkirk.

'The key to achieving this success,' he told them, 'is the U-Boat battle in the Atlantic and the destruction of the RAF.'

The bad news of the day was that Jagdgeschwader 26 had left for a new base. They had been re-assigned back to Dortmund in Germany to help defend against attacks by British bombers.

The role of Kampfgeschwader 55 would be to bomb the RAF airports. To help achieve this they would be supported by fighters from Jagdgeschwader 2, nicknamed the Richthofen group, based at Evreux, an Airport well to the west of Paris. This support would be for missions against the south west of England.

When attacking targets in the south east of England they would be supported by the highly successful Jagdgeschwader 52 Me 109's, based at Le Touquet.

This would give them more support while across the channel as the fighters would have less distance to fly to get over English territory.

They were also told that plans were being made to move the Richthofens to a forward fighter base at Cherbourg. From there they could count on the best support possible from the German fighter squadrons as they took the fight across the Channel.

Next came news of the mission for Monday.

A big curtain was drawn back along the wall behind the Oberleutnant to reveal a map of the south of England. On the map, pins had been placed with coloured strings indicating the route they would be taking on tomorrow's mission.

The plan was to fly north across Paris, cross the French coast at Dieppe and then the south coast of England near Brighton, flying over Maidstone and then on to attack the RAF base at Eastchurch in Kent on the Isle of Sheppey.

The base was being used by the RAF to harass German coastal traffic and was also being used as a base to attack the build-up of troops near the Channel coast. As such it was a prime target for the Luftwaffe.

Support for this mission would come from the fighters based at Le Touquet, just north of Dieppe. Air reconnaissance photographs of the base were handed around to the pilots and navigators, together with maps, which showed the route each crew would take. Clear skies were forecast for the morning and take off was planned for 5am. The whole Gruppe would be involved, and as newer Heinkels had been delivered during the day, it meant 30 planes would be taking to the sky early next morning.

It was confirmed they would all be carrying 8, 250 kilogram, bombs on this raid to try and cause the most damage possible to the base. The main targets were the control tower, hangars and runway. Once the raid was completed the Gruppe would circle out into the Channel and regain the French coast as soon as possible, before heading back to base.

Once the briefing was over, Bernhard headed out into the evening light to look at his plane and check all was well. Ground crews were busy repairing damage, carrying out engine checks and loading the bombs into the bomb bays. The bombs would not be armed until the morning, just before takeoff.

Bernhard had a chat with the maintenance crew and then headed back to his billet to write his weekly letter home and fill in his diary.

He had a lot to tell.

Once he was safely back in his room and the blackout curtains were fixed in place he lit a candle on the table next to his bed and took out the small case he took wherever he went. He opened the case and took out the fountain pen his mother had given him on his 18th birthday, a bottle of his favourite purple ink and some blue paper. He also took out his diary but the letter home was the first priority.

In a cultured hand, he began his letter.

Dear Mutter and Vater

Life continues to be good here in France, especially now that the French have surrendered. The war goes well. I have excellent new accommodation near Paris and today we visited the city for the first time.

I saw Versailles and the Eiffel Tower and drank coffee in a real French Cafe on the Champs Elysees. I even saw Adolf Hitler who was taking a tour of the French capital. If it wasn't for the uniforms you could have forgotten we are at war.

I even had the chance to see a film in a Parisian Theatre. The girls here are really beautiful and full of smiles for the conquering heroes, I think we have almost been accepted now peace has come to France. I had some pictures taken which I will send on to you as soon as they are developed.

I have a busy time ahead so may not be able to write again for a few days, but as you know I will try and keep in touch as best I can.

I hope you are both well and Greta is being a good daughter. Give the Wolf a pat from me, I can't wait to take him for a walk in the forest next time I am home. Willie is well and sends his regards too. He is a good friend.

Love to you both

Your Son

Bernhard x

He carefully folded the letter and slipped it into an envelope. He sealed it and wrote their address on the front and then put it in a tray on his table to be posted the next day.

He knew it would be censored which is why he was careful what to mention in the letter and he kept clear of the tragedy he had witnessed the day before. He hoped he had said nothing confidential or sensitive and his parents would get his note in its entirety.

With an early start ahead, he set his faithful old alarm clock for 3.55am. He knew he couldn't oversleep as the crew were all woken an hour before take-off anyway but he liked to be awake when the knock came and get up on his terms not those of the Luftwaffe.

He got himself ready for bed and he fell asleep as soon as his head hit the pillow.

Magloch House, Scotland

The war seemed a million miles away for Rachel and her friends.

Since setting off from the kitchen after breakfast, the girls, with Mary's guidance, had explored the huge grounds of the Magloch House Estate, sat on a horse for the first time, driven a carriage, picnicked on a Scottish Hillside amongst beautiful heather and under a clear blue sky, laughed, played and generally had a thoroughly good time.

They had returned to the house at around 5pm, just in time for tea. Cook had a lamb stew ready for the girls, complete with homemade dumplings. This was followed by fresh fruit.

At 7pm on the dot, Mary suggested it was time for them to go back to their room and get ready for bed. There were no complaints.

As they walked back along the hallway, above the large dining room, they looked down and saw the Lady and Gentleman enjoying their evening meal. Rachel, driven by gratitude, shouted, 'thank you!'

The lady stopped, the fork halfway to her mouth, and slowly looked around.

She looked up at the girls, smiled and nodded and then went back to her meal. Mary ushered the girls along the corridor towards their room.

When they got back to their room they found more new clothes waiting for them, as well as bowls of fruit and sweets and jugs of lemonade and water for them to enjoy. There was also a shelf of books for them to read. Mary sat them down and advised that they never do anything like that again.

'The family like their peace and quiet when they are having their meal,' she told them.

The girls apologised and Mary left them to get ready for bed.

The girls were flabbergasted by the whole experience. They had never seen such wealth or beauty. They got into their new bed clothes, enjoyed their new toiletries and then climbed into bed and chatted away about the day's adventures.

Mary had told them that the house owners were part of a family that made wallpaper and that they were very wealthy. They had one son, but he had been killed in the war. They were now too old to have any more children. The house had become a sad place and they were completely focused on their business. When the request had come along to help with the evacuees they had decided to take in a couple of girls, but had seen how close the three friends were, so had agreed to take them all.

While they were happy for the girls to stay there, they didn't want to be involved in looking after them, so had employed Mary to do that for them. Mary was related to Cook so when news of the position of Nanny came along, she quickly applied, and on Cook's recommendation was taken on.

The girls were allowed the run of the grounds and to eat their meals with the servants but they weren't allowed in the main house except on a Sunday, starting next Sunday, when they would be expected to go to church with the Lady and Master of the house and join them for their evening meal. Mary advised them that they should speak only when spoken too.

At 9.30pm Mary came back and wished them all sweet dreams. She turned the lights out and left the girls alone with their thoughts.

As she lay in her bed, close to sleep, Rachel suddenly realised she hadn't thought of her family back in Guernsey at all during the day. Mary had cleverly made sure the conversation never turned to home, it was all focused on Magloch House, what was happening here and now, and what they would be doing, going forward. They had never looked back.

Then the tears came.

How could she forget them so easily? What had they been doing all day? Were they all well? Had the Germans attacked? So many questions went through her head. She was upset and promised herself that she would write a letter home the next day to tell them that she was safe and well.

With that comforting thought she fell into a deep sleep.

In the bottom of the wardrobe her small case lay empty. It had been opened and all of her clothes packed away or discarded by Mary, if she had felt they were too old and worn to keep. The letter from her father now lay unopened on the cupboard opposite the end of her bed.

Chapter 6 – Monday 24th June 1940

In the News

French and Italians sign an Armistice
British Commandos attack Pas de Calais
Churchill assured French Fleet will not be used against the British
U-Boat war continues in the Atlantic

Villacoublay, Paris, France

The excitement of victory over France was short lived and now it was business as usual at Villacoublay.

Somehow Bernhard ate some breakfast before getting himself ready for the mission. He managed some sausage and egg with some black bread, then headed off to the loo for one last "rest" before takeoff. One thing that the new Heinkel 111 didn't have was a toilet.

Once he was kitted up in his flying suit and helmet he walked out to the tarmac and kicked all of the tyres of his plane. The rest of the crew watched and Willie shouted. 'Give it a kick from me!'

They all laughed as they had done on every previous mission. Superstition and routine were vital for their sanity and if doing this before each trip got them home safe then that was fine for all concerned.

With the ritual complete it was down to business. Bernhard *"Schwein gehabt"* Schmitt, as he had become known, signed a form handed to him by the chief of the ground crew. That put the plane firmly in his hands and detailed all of the repairs that had been carried out. They climbed on board and ran through a quick system check.

There was never enough time for all the checks recommended in the "instruction book".

At 5am precisely, German time, a flare shot up from the control tower and 30 Heinkel 111s and a dozen Dornier 'flying pencils' burst into life with a huge roar and one by one they started to taxi out on to the runway.

As the runway at Villacoublay was quite wide the planes took off in staggered pairs, each pair waiting until the pair in front had cleared the runway before starting their take off runs. The planes got away safely and circled around above the runway gaining height and getting into group formation.

With another flare launched this time from the group leader they headed north towards the coast and the English Channel. Flying at 5,000 metres, they could clearly see the English coast ahead of them even before they reached the French coast.

From that height, it appeared a very narrow stretch of water.

Soon they were joined by groups of Me 109's flying above and below them, providing a protective screen against British fighters.

Below them, the English radar had already picked up the flotilla of bombers and fighters. Hurricanes and Spitfires from 11 Group defending the south west of the UK were being scrambled even before the German bombers had reached the coast.

The British were soon engaging the Me 109's and a large dog fight was taking place all around the bombers. When possible, Bernhard's machine gunners would open up when an English fighter got in range but by and large they were being kept busy by the Me 109's.

More British fighters were quickly on the scene and some of them were starting to get through to the bombers. Many began to take hits and a few even had to turn around with smoke trailing from damaged engines.

Bernhard's luck held and he pressed on towards the English coast. There were still around 30 bombers in the air and, as many of the British fighters had to turn back to refuel and re-arm, they seemed to enjoy some respite. Then, as they crossed the Sussex coast, more Hurricanes joined them in battle and again they were subjected to a vicious attack. With many of their own fighters out of the fray through lack of ammunition and fuel they were to all intents and purposes on their own, and their losses started to mount.

Guernsey

After such a good weekend and some quality time with his family, work came as a bit of a shock to Laurence. The day dawned bright and clear again and it was tempting just to say, *to hell with it* and stay home. As always, money and of course his conscientiousness were the drivers.

Normality also seemed vital for the children as well as themselves. In fact, normality was a good word. The smoke had cleared over Cherbourg and for a while you could imagine that the world was at peace and nothing was amiss.

The day's papers told a slightly different story, if you ignored the headlines. 'The Island settles down again' was the banner cry, and if you ignored the details you could imagine just that. The cinemas were reopening and Laurence decided to treat his family to a trip to the North Cinema that evening to see the Marx Brothers starring in a film called, "At the Circus".

There was already a large tomato boat in the harbour to fill, so he was busy all day coordinating the exports of the bumper crop that was a direct result of all of the fine weather.

The fruit was ripening fast and had to be picked and shipped as quickly as possible. Two more tomato boats were also scheduled for the next day. He noted from the manifests that very few passengers were due to travel.

The day flew by as the constant flow of paper work distracted him from reality. Tea flowed too, helping him concentrate on the task at hand. Lunch was a hurried sandwich which Lily had packed for him that morning, and he barely had time to look at the office paper and take in the news. In fact, that Monday he worked a full 10-hour day to try and keep on top of the paperwork.

Knowing it would be a full day, and he might miss his bus home, he had ridden his bike in to work, so, at just after 6pm, once all the paperwork was done, Laurence rode his bike home. Wearing his bicycle clips and a pair of gloves he cycled along the front, just as the tomato boat, stuffed full with 45,000 chip baskets full of Guernsey's finest produce, made its way north towards England, the same direction in which he was cycling.

Early in the morning, Lily had walked with Ma and the children down to the Bridge to collect a paper. Laurence had asked her to make the journey over breakfast, as he knew there would be a good chance he would be late home.

The women had looked around the shops to see what they could find to vary their diet a bit and Lily had been lucky to find some French cheese.

That will be ideal, she thought and of course she also thought they wouldn't be getting much more of that now that France was occupied. She had also been told that milk deliveries would be stopping but they tended to get their milk from Luff's anyway. A banner advert in the paper declared that "Luff's are Business as Usual".

Lily had left Ma with the kids after their visit to the shops to give her the chance to walk down to Bert Martel's vinery in the Braye Road.

As Tony had suggested he was on his own, picking tomatoes as fast as he could, and even Lily's untrained eye could see there were too many red tomatoes on the vines and that they would probably go to waste.

Lily introduced herself and before she knew what was happening Bert was showing her how to pick a tomato and how they were packed and sorted. She agreed to spend a few hours with him to help with the workload and soon she was in the swing of it, filling chip baskets faster than Bert was. She loved the smell of the tomatoes and her fingers were soon green, something that would be difficult to shift, even with a good scrub in carbolic soap.

After three hours' solid work, a grateful Bert gave her a bag of tomatoes to take home and booked her time in his diary ready to pay her at the end of the week. He told her she could come back whenever she wanted and they agreed she would try and get there as often as she could.

With that she walked back to her mother's house, collected the kids, and walked home to get ready for their evening out.

As soon as Laurence arrived home he freshened up, changed his shirt and put on a nice blazer before the family all headed towards the Bridge for the evening showing at the North Cinema. Lily had fed the children and made him another sandwich, cheese and tomato, which he ate on the way to the cinema as they were a bit tight for time. It was all a bit of a rush but he knew the Marx Brothers would make it worth their while.

Lily told him all about her day on the way to the cinema. He couldn't believe how excited she was about her job and knew she would be down there again as soon as possible.

They settled down in the Cinema after standing for the National Anthem and got ready for the main event.

Magloch House, Scotland

Rachel and her friends had woken to a beautiful summer's day and they rushed off to the bathroom to get themselves ready for the adventures that lay ahead. In the night, her father's letter had slipped down flat on top of the cupboard and had gone unnoticed by Rachel in her mad rush to get ready

After an early breakfast of creamy porridge, they were soon down at the stables helping to muck out the horses and bring in fresh bedding. All of the staff had quickly taken to the polite Guernsey girls even though a few struggled to understand their accents, just as the girls struggled to understand the local's Scottish lilt.

However, the girls knew their arduous work would be rewarded as Mary had promised them a proper riding lesson later in the morning.

The chosen horse was an old grey mare which Mary called Star. Christine was allowed to go first and after helping her into the saddle, Mary walked her around the paddock. Julie and Rachel looked on from behind the fence as gradually Christine's nerves settled down and under Mary's expert tutelage she became more confident in the saddle.

The lesson ended with a short trot before Mary helped her down and it was Rachel's turn in the saddle. Rachel had been pleased that Christine had gone first as she had been quite nervous about riding such a big creature but when she saw the smile on Christine's face she couldn't wait to get on the quiet grey horse and have her turn.

The training went on until noon with each of the girls getting three rides each. Then Mary declared they had all done well and that it was time for lunch.

As if by magic Mary produced a hearty ploughman's lunch. Rachel had never seen so much cheese and was so hungry that she cleared her plate and would have asked for more if she hadn't been still a little shy in her new surroundings. After everything was cleared away they headed out again, this time in the carriage.

Mary drove them down to a small lake, or loch as she called it, and there, tied up at the end of a small pier, was a dinghy. After tethering Jock to a post near the pier, they clambered in to the boat and before long Mary was rowing them out into the middle of the loch. The surface was mirror flat and after a while she stopped rowing and let the water around them settle.

It was so still and they all sat in awe of the beautiful surroundings, lulled by the warmth and the gentle lapping of the water against the side of the dinghy. High above them a large bird, which Mary assured them was an eagle, circled in the warm air. Occasionally a fish would jump and make a splash. One jumped out of the water so close it made the girls jump.

'Would you like to try fishing one day?' Mary asked.

'Yes please,' they all replied in chorus.

Mary smiled and promised to make the arrangements for a fishing trip.

After thirty minutes or so Mary picked up the oars and rowed them back to the pier. It had been a fantastic experience for them all. In the carriage on the way back they all talked about the type of fish they would catch and if Cook would prepare it for them for tea. Mary told tales of giant trout and salmon, fish the girls had never heard of.

Rachel noticed her friends were starting to get more colour in their cheeks and looked fitter and healthier than they had been before. She mentioned it to Mary and she insisted it was the Scottish air.

As they came back into the stable yard, Rachel spotted a man in a skirt. She giggled and pointed him out to Mary. Mary shushed her quite sharply. "Why, have you never seen a kilt before?' she asked.

'No never.' Rachel replied. 'Who is that man?'

'That's Young Jack, the Masters Gillie,' said Mary and explained that a Gillie was the man in charge of all of the animals and any hunting and fishing that took place on the Estate.

'If the Gentlemen want to go shooting or fishing, Young Jack goes with them to make sure everything is done safely and properly.'

Young Jack gave them a wave and Mary waved back. Rachel noticed she seemed very enthusiastic with her waving. She caught Rachel watching her and blushed. *I think she likes Young Jack*, she thought with a knowing smile.

Rachel asked her why he was called Young Jack. Mary explained that his father had been called Jack and was the Gillie before him. Old Jack had died a couple of years ago in a climbing accident and Young Jack had inherited the role.

Once they were back in the house and they had taken off their boots, the girls gathered around the big table in the kitchen.

They all helped peel some potatoes and carrots while the others prepared the meat and a vegetable Rachel had never seen before, which she later discovered to be a turnip.

After the food was cooked, the girls, together with Mary and a couple of other staff enjoyed another hearty meal together, overseen by Cook. Rachel couldn't believe how hungry she was and how much food she could eat. Even Mary wondered where the small girl from Guernsey put all of her food.

Hollow legs, she mused with a smile on her face

After another lovely evening with her friends, having taken a walk around the gardens before it got dark, Rachel was all too soon back in her new bed and sound asleep. The promise to write her letter home forgotten.

The Skies above Kent

Bernhard was now getting very worried. German fighters were almost non-existent and he could hear his own crew fiercely defending the plane against the onslaught of the British Hurricanes. The Heinkels and Dorniers flew in a tight formation, trying to provide covering fire for each other. The Hurricanes, however, seemed able to find blind spots in the formation and every few minutes it seemed another plane would fall from the safety of the group and spiral towards the hard earth below.

The target was close now, he could make out the aerodrome and began to line up his plane on the target. Suddenly the skies were clear of fighters and for a moment he thought they were safe.

Then suddenly the sky around him erupted with flak as shells exploded amongst his Heinkels from the ground defences.

He experienced, for the first time over England, the pitter patter of shrapnel bouncing off his aircraft and the glass canopy which surrounded him. He thought it sounded a bit like heavy rain which made him wish there had been a few rain clouds in the sky.

Suddenly one of the *Gruppe* took a direct hit and exploded, damaging another Heinkel flying alongside. Once again, the *Gruppe* shrank in numbers but now the target was in range.

Determination and concentration took over as well as a strong burst of adrenalin. Willie took his place in the bomb aimer's position and began a countdown to the drop point. He urged Bernhard to move slightly to starboard and then called '*Feuer Frei!*'

Bernhard reached up and pulled the bomb release lever and felt the eight massive bombs fall away. The plane suddenly lurch higher into the sky, free of its load. He quickly assessed his position in the *Gruppe* and, seeing a clear path, turned to starboard and threw the plane into a steep dive.

The anti-aircraft shells were now exploding high above him and the extra speed was taking him quickly away from the chaotic skies above the aerodrome.

Unbeknown to Bernhard his bombs had dropped in a perfect line across the Eastchurch runway. The last in the stack had landed next to the base of the control tower destroying a gun emplacement and causing some damage to the tower itself. They would need a lot of replacement glass, Kai would joke with him later!

As the battle above the airport thinned out, each surviving Heinkel and Dornier broke for home in different directions. A few were unlucky and were spotted by British fighters but most made it across the coast and like Bernhard enjoyed a relatively safe journey home.

Eastchurch suffered some damage and a few losses to personnel, particularly amongst the gun crews and one unlucky ambulance crew. However, thanks to the remarkable resilience of the British, it would be operational again the following day.

German losses were high, six Heinkels and two Dorniers were shot down and six more were badly damaged. They also lost two Messerschmitts and in total they lost 34 crewmen, though some were seen bailing out over England. The British lost three Hurricanes, only one went down with its pilot.

Bernhard's landing was loudly applauded by his crew as usual, and after the engines had stopped turning, he climbed out of the plane. Bernhard took a tour around his Heinkel to check for damage. Apart from a few obvious scratches caused by the shrapnel it looked unscathed. His *schwein gehabt* (lucky dog) nickname had proved right yet again.

He then made his way, with Willie and the three K's, to de-briefing. As he walked his mind went to the parachutes he had seen gently gliding down and in a way, he envied the survivors. At least they were safe and would play no further part in this terrible war.

After a very subdued the de-briefing, the Oberleutnant took Bernhard to one side and told him a promotion was coming through for him. They had recognised his leadership abilities and the results of his sorties had been good. He was being recommended for promotion to Stabsfeldwebel (Warrant Officer).

Bernhard thanked him profusely and the Oberleutnant shook his hand and wished him continued success.

He rushed off to tell Willie his good news.

North Cinema, Guernsey

They say laughter is infectious and it certainly seemed to be the case in the North Cinema that evening. Although only half full, the laughter at times seemed to border on hysteria, and many were still in fits of laughter as they walked out of the cinema. Being mid-summer, it was still light and the family held hands as they walked home across the Bridge reminding each other of their favourite bits in the film. Much of it was about the Gorilla that stole the show and of course Groucho's song about Lydia the Tattooed Lady, which they all tried to sing.

When they got home the children were packed off to bed straight away, it was way past their normal bed time. The kettle was put on for a cup of Horlicks before bed. Lily and Laurence curled up on the sofa with their drinks and chatted about their lovely evening. They turned the radio on to the Home Service and Laurence finally got to read the paper. They chatted about going to the Cinema again but decided there was nothing on that they could take the children to.

The Lyric had "Over the Moon", the Gaumont had "Untamed" and the Regal had "The Great Victor Herbert". Lily pulled a face at that one so all thoughts of the cinema were forgotten.

Lily mentioned it was strange without Rachel, and they chatted about what she might be doing and hoped she was safe. There had been little mention of air raids lately, and they hoped she would be far away from any potential danger.

They were both very tired after their busy days, so by 10.30pm they decided it was time for bed.

It almost felt as if the Stars headline, "Island Settles Down Again" was true but underlying that statement was a cold truth.

What were the islanders settling down to?

Villacoublay, Paris, France

The afternoon had passed quite quickly for Bernhard with routine paperwork, some lunch, airplane checks and some relaxation time in the deckchair with Greif, his faithful dog. Aircrews were busy working on several of the planes as he was called back for an early evening briefing. He assumed it would be about a mission the following day, but as soon as they walked in they knew this would be different. A stranger was standing next to the Oberleutnant and he waited until everyone had settled down before starting the briefing.

The Oberleutnant introduced him as Major Rudolph Becker.

The Major thanked Oberleutnant Holstein for letting him speak and started to talk about the next mission which would be a raid on RAF Debden in Essex, north of London. The route they would take was laid out on the large map on the wall and the navigators furiously jotted down the route and timings for the journey.

There was little of note to worry about and several of the pilots glanced at each other, wondering why this man was giving the briefing instead of the Oberleutnant. Then he dropped the bombshell, take off would be at midnight.

There was a murmur around the room loud enough for the Oberleutnant to shout 'Silence!' at them.

Once everyone had settled down the Major continued. He explained that he was a night fighter pilot and had been flying at night since the war had begun. He, and a colleague from his Nachtjagdgeschwader 3 group, would be escorting two Kettes of Bernhard's, Kampfgeschwader 55.

As this was their first night mission, the night fighters would lead the Kampfgeschwader 55 crews to the target and protect them in case they were attacked by British night fighters.

He then went through the main types of British night fighters they might face. These included the Boulton Paul Defiant, which tended to attack from below, as they had a gun turret mounted just behind the pilot's seat and the twin engine Bristol Blenheim Mk 1F. The latter also had a dorsal mounted turret but unlike the Defiant it had a wing mounted machine gun so could also attack head on.

All of the pilots had some experience of the principles of night bombing but up until now none of them had actually been involved in any night time missions. nor had come across a Defiant in combat, though some knew of the Blenheim.

The Major went on to talk about the guidance system that would be used on the raid. The system was called *Knickebein* which consisted of two radio beams which were centred over the target. The planes were vectored to follow one of the beams and when they crossed the intersecting beam they would drop their bombs, in this case, directly over RAF Debden.

The Oberleutnant took over the briefing and told them that their planes had been fitted with the *Knickebein* receivers. He then announced who would be taking part in the raid and Bernhard was told he would be leading the second Kette.

He could feel his heart beating in his chest at the thought of flying across England in the dark and making it back to Villacoublay safely. He glanced at Willie who looked like he was in a state of shock.

'You'll be fine,' he whispered to him.

After questions, the briefing was called to a close, the Navigators were asked to stay behind and it was suggested the others get some sleep. The call would come at 11pm.

Bernhard went to his billet and set his alarm for 10.55. He fell into a restless sleep.

In his dreams, he was flying through a black sky, lights flashed all around him. Suddenly his plane was hit and he was falling, falling ….

He woke in a pool of sweat and realised it was 10.50pm. He flicked his alarm off and got out of his bunk.

Still dressed from the briefing he washed his face and put his flying gear on. Willie was also up and ready to go, he had been running through the plans for the raid in his head and couldn't sleep.

When they met up outside their billet, he told Bernhard that after the briefing they had been given some last minutes instructions and training by the Major in their Heinkel running through all the details of the *Knickebein* system and how it worked.

He was now confident they would be fine and he assured Bernhard he knew how to use the system and could get them home. Bernhard had been worrying about how they would get back and Willie explained that a Lorenz system had been installed at Villacoublay which would enable him to direct Bernhard into the airport safely, even in complete darkness.

'As long as you can get us within 20 miles of Villacoublay, I'll bring you home.' Willie said confidently

Bernhard was a little nervous on how it might all work but had faith in Willie, and his crew. They would be alright.

At 11.45 they were in their planes and taxiing to the end of the runway. The sky was clear and there was hardly a breath of wind. The ground crews had loaded the planes with 8 bombs each and they were planning on doing as much damage as possible to the RAF facilities and fighters based in Debden.

Chapter 7 – Tuesday 25th June 1940
In the News

Hitler orders all German flags flown and church bells rung to celebrate their success in Europe.
German troops begin preparation for the invasion of Britain

Villacoublay, France

As the clock passed midnight a bright flare lit up the sky and a line of trucks turned their headlights on to light up the runway. Bernhard and the other two pilots in his Kette waited for the first three planes to take off. Once they had disappeared into the darkness Bernhard lined his Heinkel 111 up on the runway. Without a pause, he pushed the throttles to full power and the tremendous roar of the twin Daimler Benz engines filled his ears as they powered down the runway and took off.

He was barely 100 metres off the ground when the truck lights turned off and they were heading up into a cloudless night sky. The moon was just past full and as they turned north they could clearly see the River Seine winding its way through Paris, which was under a strict black out.

As they gained height, in the distance, they could see the moonlight reflecting off the Channel.

The plan was that they would fly up the French/Belgium coast towards the North Sea and then turn north west, pick up the *Knickebein* signal, and then follow it to RAF Debden. Another signal would then appear when it was time to drop their payload.

There was hardly a light to be seen on the ground as they droned up the coast. Bernhard was glued to the spectacular views, paying attention to his headphones and the odd course direction being passed to him by Willie, when suddenly the moon disappeared.

Not 100 metres from him, the impressive shape of a twin-engine Messerschmitt BF 110 had appeared. The fact it had sneaked up on him and his crew so easily scared him to his core as he knew the British had night fighters too. A red light flickered from the back of the fighter, which was the agreed follow me signal and they started to angle north to pick up the beam from the Knickebein station in Kleve.

'Signal acquired.' Willie reported.

With another confirmation flash from the Messerschmitt, they banked to port and began their approach to RAF Debden. They were still well out over the North Sea but they could see the land ahead shrouded in darkness.

As they crossed the coast the Messerschmitt suddenly veered off, Willie told Bernhard that a British Blenheim had been detected. The Major had gone off in pursuit.

The other Nachtjagdgeschwader 3 fighter had stayed with the first Kette up ahead but for now Bernhard and his Kette were on their own.

Down below them they spotted tracer fire as the dogfight in the dark took place, but they held their course and continued to follow the signal from the Knickebein sytem.

As they crossed the coast a few search lights started to light up the sky, the British radar had no doubt detected them. One of the three planes up in front was caught in the light and soon flak was bursting around them. He had seen flak in the daytime, and was used to the black puffs of smoke and the rattle of shrapnel hitting the plane, but seeing the flashes in the dark was far more unnerving.

He knew the chances of being hit by flak were small and while the British guns were firing at them, he didn't have to worry about night fighters.

As they crossed the coast Bernhard told Willie to arm the bombs.
They had been over land for about ten minutes and were flying at 3,000 metres. Bernhard knew it wouldn't be long before they would be over the target. He reached up and grabbed hold of the bomb release lever.

'Knickebein acquired.' Willie reported and tapped him on the shoulder for good measure.

He had been so focused Willie's voice made him jump.

Bernhard pulled the bomb release lever which released the 8 bombs at 3 second intervals. He turned around just in time to see the last of the bombs fall away from its location behind him.

The bombs fell tail first, but the fins soon corrected their flight into the right nose down attitude for their short but terrible fall to earth.

As planned, as soon as the bombs were away, they banked to starboard and climbed away into the night sky, still in formation. As they turned, Willie from his position in the waist of the plane, reported that he saw explosions on the ground but he could not tell if the target had been hit. A reconnaissance mission would fly over later in the day to see what the results of the raid had been.

Soon they were back over the sea and retracing their route until they were safely over German occupied territory. The night fighters, who had rejoined them after the bombing run, waggled their wings and flew off to their base while Willie concentrated on navigating their Kette back to Villacoublay.

Bernhard would only be happy when they were back on the ground but he had to admit his first experience of night bombing had been rather surreal. They had not been chased by any Hurricane's, had experienced very little flak and of course had the protection of the night fighters. This had all added up to a sense of security which made him believe this was the way they should operate in future. He made a mental note to tell the Oberleutnant that in the de-briefing.

Thanks to the bright moon and the clear sky, Willie's job was made a lot easier on the way home, as the River Seine gave him a good marker for the run into Villacoublay but he was determined to use the Lorenz system and once he picked up the signal he guided Bernhard down towards the runway.

All of the planes now had red tail lights on to avoid the potential for collisions and at about 5 miles out he spotted a distant flare and once again the truck lights lit the runway as the first Kette arrived back home.

Once those three Heinkels were all safely down, the lights blinked off and Bernhard depended on guidance from Willie until a second flare arched into the sky and the truck lights came back on.

Within minutes they were down, the usual applause ringing around the plane from the happy crew. The lights went out as soon as the third plane touched down and a few men with hand held lamps guided the planes back to their stands.

Bernhard breathed a sigh of relief as they wriggled down through the hatch back on to the concrete. He gave Willie a huge hug and arm in arm they walked back to the tower and de-briefing. Obviously without any visual results to talk about, the report was more about how the technical aspects of the mission.

Bernhard told the Oberleutnant how smoothly it had gone and all of the crews agreed it was a relatively easy mission. The security offered by the Messerschmitt BF 110's had been an added bonus.

The Oberleutnant suggested they get some sleep and prepare for more missions like this, dependent on the results of the raid. He also mentioned to Bernhard that there was a special delivery waiting for him in his billet.

Curious, he headed back to his room.

An envelope, with a swastika in the corner sat on his desk. He opened it and inside was a letter confirming his promotion. The envelope also contained the badges associated with his new rank. Shoulder flashes, collar badges and the black badge with the four wings for the sleeves of his flight suit were all included.

He got out his diary and noted his promotion. He then recorded the detail of the raid on RAF Debden. He decided he would write a letter home after he had got some sleep.

He got undressed and lay on his cot. It was too warm for bed covers. Tiredness washed over him and his last thought before he dropped off to sleep was who he could get to sew on his new flashes.

This time there were no nightmares and he slept soundly until 6am when he was woken by the noise of the base getting ready for another busy day.

Guernsey

The day dawned bright again. There would be no respite as regards the tomato exports. Lily would be off early picking tomatoes for her new employer and Laurence would be working hard ensuring they were being shipped to the right places.

The newspapers emphasised the importance of getting Guernsey back to work and there were assurances that there were adequate supplies for the islanders and that would continue for the foreseeable future. Bacon and butter were unrationed.

Almost as an aside it was reported that the hostilities between France and Germany were over. The guns in Europe were silent and Britain stood alone. A Franco Italian armistice was also reported in the press as were bombing raids on London.

Perhaps people thought that would be the end of it. Apart from the empty houses all seemed normal. 100,000 chips of tomatoes were due to be exported again today and business was good.

The only negative on the home front was a press report stating that there would be no buses this Sunday as the island tried to make savings on fuel.

Work was bordering on the boring for Laurence, and the first cup of tea of the day at 9.30am gave him a welcome moment of respite. The queues of trucks outside seemed never ending and in reality, they were. As soon as one unloaded it was driven back to the vinery to be refilled.

During the morning, Harold, one of his colleagues in the band, had popped in to tell him they had a booking at the Royal Hotel on Thursday night. Not only were the cinemas now open but so to were the dance halls.

He was really pleased to be able to get his drumsticks out again and earn some extra money for the family. Things were getting back to normal.

In contrast, Lily was enjoying her new job. She loved the camaraderie of her fellow pickers, something she had rarely experienced. Bert had managed to get a few more staff overnight, from the pub apparently, but because Lily had been first to his aid he put her in charge. As such she was suddenly a foreman, and her wage packet was going to be slightly more, which made her smile even more.

It didn't take long for the men to realise why Bert had chosen Lily as she was the fastest picker amongst them and never stopped to rest the whole day.

She even organised their lunchtimes to make sure work never stopped. Bert was very happy as another truck full of chip baskets each filled with his precious red fruit left the vinery on the first leg of its journey to England.

On top of the extra money, Lily knew she would be able to take home as many tomatoes as she wanted, which would help with the food bill. She was already planning several different soups and meals involving tomatoes. She missed the children but she had to admit her work had taken her mind off worrying about Rachel and the war.

She had also learned how to grade the tomatoes. The best and usually the biggest were called pinks, then in size terms they went down to yellows, whites, blues and finally the smallest and least valuable were the greens. Tissue paper lined the chip baskets and a couple of the guys hammered the lids on once they were full.

She was just hanging up her apron when Tony gave her a shout as he was walking across to his truck to take the last load of chip baskets to the harbour.

'Fancy a lift to the town love? You can meet up with your husband and go home together.'

She was really excited at the thought as she had hardly ever been in a car and never in a truck.

'Yes please,' she replied excitedly.

Tony had to help her up the steps into the truck cab as she was so short and her legs could barely reach the first step. As she settled in the cab, she realised her hands were still green and smelled strongly of tomatoes. She also felt a bit strange sitting next to Tony who she hardly knew.

She turned to Tony. 'Can I sit in the back of the truck? I'd love to do that and feel the wind in my hair.'

'Sure,' he replied. He helped her back out of the cab and then grabbed a few boxes to create a makeshift set of steps to help her climb up into the back and she made herself comfortable on the chip baskets.

Hopefully Laurence won't mind me turning up out of the blue, she thought.
Soon they were off on their way to St Peter Port. On the journey they passed her house which brought a smile to her face. She felt that life was good and things were going well, apart from missing Rachel of course.

Maybe we made the wrong decision, she thought.

Villacoublay, Paris, France

Bernhard got dressed before most of the other crews were awake and took a stroll around the airport perimeter. He knew he would be flying again today but didn't know what the target was going to be. As he walked, a Dornier took off, *no doubt* he thought, *to do some reconnaissance on their night time raid.*

If they were sent up again today he hoped that it wasn't going to be Dover or anywhere so well defended. In his heart, he prayed that they might just be sent on night missions in future.

After his walk, he made his way back to the officer's mess where breakfast was waiting for him. He drank strong black coffee and ate toast and jam followed by eggs and ham. He even enjoyed a croissant brought in, no doubt, from a local French Patisserie.

Breakfast was so important to Bernhard and the rest of the crews as they were never sure when they would eat again during the day. As usual, he took an extra roll which he would place in his flight suit to keep him going whilst in the air.

By 8am he was well fed and rested and raring to go. He strode in to the briefing room and sat next to Max who he had got to know after the de-briefing session for the morning raid the previous day. They shook hands and got out their note pads ready to hear what plans the Luftwaffe had for them that day.

To his relief, he heard that they would be flying down to the west coast of France to harass the last remaining pockets of troops whom the allies were trying to evacuate from France. With the French surrender a few days before, this should be as easy a mission as you could get.

They had a couple of hours before the mission so Bernhard took Greif for a walk and Max came along with them for some exercise. Bernhard and Max chatted of home and found out a lot more about each other. Bernhard discovered Max had followed a similar route to where they were now. He had been shot down once over Poland but had managed to bail out along with all of his crew. They considered him a lucky pilot too.

Much of Max's work recently had been centred on the observation and photography of enemy positions and up until the last week he had seen little action.

Once again, a mixed group of 6 Heinkels and 3 Dorniers would be on today's mission but this time they would be flying in their own groups. The Heinkels would go in low while the Dorniers would bomb from three thousand metres.

It had been a long time since Bernhard had seen the inside of a Dornier so he asked Max for a tour. Max was delighted to show his new friend around his plane so they headed over to the hastily repaired Dornier and climbed into the cockpit.

His first impression was the apparent height difference between the pilot's position in the DO 17 and that of his Heinkel 111. The view was excellent but he didn't feel as exposed as he usually felt in his "greenhouse". The positions for the 4 crewmen were much closer than in the Heinkel and he felt that they could work together much better. As he thought about the differences, he didn't feel that the Dornier had the defensive capabilities that his Heinkel had. He was happy to leave Max in his Dornier and head back to his own plane.

At 11am precisely a flare went up and engines were started across the airfield. The Heinkels were first up and circled Villacoublay until the Dorniers joined them at 2,000 metres above Paris. They then headed south west towards the coast, then turned south in search of their targets around Bayonne.

The Dorniers climbed higher as the Heinkels circled away and descended ready for their low-level bombing run.

St Peter Port, Guernsey

Laurence was keen to get home. Lily had been working in the greenhouses all day and he missed her desperately.

He popped out of the office to look at the queue of lorries and pick up a few forms from the drivers. He was just walking back when he heard a familiar voice.

'Cooee, Laurie Love!'

He turned around, just in time to see his gorgeous wife jump down from the back of one of the lorries and run across to him as fast as she could.

He just had time to throw his arms wide as she leapt towards him.

'Hello, my beauty, what a lovely surprise.'

He was so pleased to see Lily happy and smiling, it was the first time he had seen her really happy and carefree since Rachel had left and he was relieved that she seemed to be coping.

After he had disentangled himself from her arms, and they had kissed, they walked hand in hand to his office.

'I thought I would come down to the docks and surprise you,' she explained. 'Tony gave me a lift in his lorry. I've never been in a lorry before,' she added excitedly.

He loved the way such little things gave her so much pleasure and he squeezed her hand.

'It's lovely to see you my dear, and to see you so happy,' he told her.

They walked into his office and Lily, spying the kettle, offered to make them a cup of tea.

For once she was so talkative, telling him about her day in the greenhouse. How she had picked tomatoes, done some grading and helped load the lorry. She also explained how Bert had made her the foreman.

She then explained how Tony had offered her a lift and how she had been so excited to be sitting in the back of a lorry.

Laurence was amazed how Lily thought being in the open back of the truck sitting on chip baskets was much more fun than it was to sit up front in the shelter of the cab.

I know where I would rather sit, he thought.

He smiled as he listened to his wife. As she talked he finished his work for the day and together, hand in hand as always, they walked down to the bus.

Laurence picked up a newspaper on the way and they sat in the sun next to the old pump on the North Esplanade as they waited for the number 10.

Soon they were sitting, on the sea side of the bus, looking out across a mirror smooth sea to the island of Herm which was drenched in the evening sun of another beautiful evening. The journey finished just a little too quickly for the happy couple. After getting off the bus, they hurried across the road into their home and were assailed by the delicious smell of a full roast meal.

After the onslaught of the kids and the usual demands for a kick around in the yard from Michael, which Laurence quietly deferred, they found a smiling Ma in the kitchen, wearing Rachel's apron while she was busy spooning meat juices from a nice-looking chicken over a tray of roast potatoes.

'I thought you would both be hungry after a full day at work so one of the chickens had to be sacrificed,' she explained.

'This is lovely Ma,' said Lily, giving her Mum a kiss on the cheek. She knew how precious the chickens were to Ma as they supplied her with all of the eggs they could ever need.

Laurence looked on happily, all seemed well in the world.

That night they enjoyed a lovely family meal and Rachel was toasted in lemonade. Even the mention of her name didn't bring the usual tears.

Later on Lily asked Laurence if he thought they had made the right decision sending her to England.

'Yes, my dear,' he replied emphatically. 'We know she is safe in England and we still don't know what will happen here.'

'If after a few months all is well, we'll send for her to come home,' he added.

Lily smiled at the thought of them all being together again.

She would sleep well that night.

West Coast of France

Bernhard and the planes from Villacoublay were hunting, starting from Brest they worked their way down the west coast. It was the last day that any hostilities with France would take place with the cease fire scheduled for 2pm. They spotted the odd vessel as they worked their way down the coast but none proved to be British Navy.

Further down the west coast the last vestiges of the evacuation was taking place in St. Jean-de-Luz but that was out of range of the pilots from Villacoublay and by 2pm they were on their way back home, flying back up the coast.

The Dorniers headed back across Brittany but Bernhard took his Heinkels further north and near the island of Ushant, west of Brest, they spotted a British Frigate heading north into the Bay of St Malo.

Willie armed the bombs and climbed down into the bomb aimer position as Bernhard lined up on the Frigate. The Frigate opened fire on them and bullets and shells were flying past them as they dived down towards the warship. Willie shouted *'Feuer Frei'* and Bernhard pulled the bomb lever and immediately banked to starboard and sped away, but not before the Heinkel vibrated with hits from the ship's guns.

The rest of his Kette followed him in but the Frigate managed to avoid all of the bombs, zig zagging wildly to confuse the bomb aimers.

Bernhard was more worried now by the vibration he was feeling through his aircraft. Kass in the waist gunner position reported smoke from the port engine. Preferring to be safe than sorry, Bernhard shut down the port engine and decided to try and make it home on one.

He ordered the rest of his Kette to press on home without him but they both refused and in formation the three planes flew over Brest and headed east towards Paris. They were flying much slower than normal and would be a tempting target for any passing enemy aircraft.

All of the gunners and navigators were on the lookout for a possible attack. The waist gunner had reported to Bernhard that they were still trailing a little smoke and he was worried that a fire might build in the engine which would spread to the wing and the fuel tanks, which were close to the fuselage.

If that happened it would be catastrophic for them all and if there was any sign of the fire spreading he would order the crew to bail out and try to get the plane down in one piece.

It wasn't long before they were lined up on the runway and he could see the emergency crews waiting for them. Then the image of Heinz Klausman, the Dornier pilot came to mind and he prayed the same thing didn't happen to them. He lowered the undercarriage but the port wheel failed to come down. He ordered the crew to prepare for a crash landing.

As he brought the plane in he cut the starboard engine just as they hit the concrete of the runway and worked to keep the plane level. The Heinkel was not blessed with great stability at the best of times and pilots had to always be alert, but now Bernhard worked himself into a sweat as they lost speed rapidly.

With the knowledge of how the Dornier reacted, he threw the plane into a starboard turn just before the port wing tip hit the ground which had the effect of keeping the wing up a little longer and reducing the last of the speed. The wing tip touched the ground and immediately dragged the plane back to the left but they stayed level and ground to a halt.

The emergency crews were there in an instant and damping down the port engine before any fire could start to spread and the crew were able to scramble out and get away from the plane quickly. Bernhard was last out and as he stood up he was mobbed by the crew, including Willie, and then they all stood back and gave him their usual round of applause.

As Willie always said. 'Any landing you can walk away from is a good landing.'

They all walked back to the tower and de-briefing but before they went inside, Bernhard looked back and said a prayer of thanks as he thought once more about Heinz Klausman.

In a way, Heinz had saved his life. If he hadn't witnessed his crash, he wouldn't have known what to do when he was in the very same situation.

Thoughts of Heinz Klausman were again uppermost in his mind later in the day when he and his colleagues turned out to salute Heinz and his crew as their bodies were taken away to be transported back to Germany where they would be laid to rest along with so many other young airmen of the Luftwaffe.

Magloch House, Scotland

Rachel had enjoyed another lovely day in Scotland.

After a hearty breakfast, they had helped in the stables again, mucking out the horses and putting in new bedding. Then they were taken on a tour of the grounds with Mary leading the way, telling them about the various plants that filled the borders of the large garden.

She also told them about the history of the house, which was around 200 years old and gave them a brief history of Scotland. The girls were fascinated as they had barely known Scotland existed before they had arrived after their evacuation.

In the afternoon, the girls had been out on the loch again, this time Young Jack had joined them to show them how to fish. They were in a slightly larger boat that jack called a skiff. It had a mast and small sail.

Jack and Mary sailed the boat and the girls trailed their hands in the cool water of the Loch, watching the amazing scenery drift by.

Rachel watched how the young couple worked together and how they spoke to each other. Each was full of smiles and she was sure romance was in the air.

Once they arrived in one of Jack's favourite fishing spots they got out the rods and took turns casting the flies out on to the lake.

The girls found it hard to learn as they weren't as strong as Jack and also tended to wobble a bit when they stood up in the boat so he would cast the rods and give them to the girls to hold. Julie was first to have a bite and nearly dropped her rod in the lake with the shock of the tug from the fish.

With Jack's help, she reeled the fish in and was rewarded with a beautiful trout which Jack pulled into the boat for her. Mary was allowed a turn and she too was lucky, adding a second large trout to their catch.

Jack declared two fish was enough and explained how important it was to not overfish the lake and make sure there were always fish for future generations.

They sailed back and Jack left them at the pier so they could all ride home in the carriage and deliver their catch to Cook in time for tea.
Cook prepared the fish, showing the girls how to gut and clean them, something Christine wasn't that keen on, but when they were served for tea they all had to agree they tasted delicious.

On the way up to their room, after supper, they had seen the Lady and Gentleman of the house entertaining several guests with a grand meal in the big hall. A lady was playing a piano and the sound was amazing. They paused for a couple of minutes and listened to the music before Mary ushered them on to their room so they could get ready for bed.

In the quiet of their room they could hear the faint sound of the piano and Rachel wished she could play an instrument like that. *I'll ask Mary if someone could teach me to play the piano,* she thought, as she dropped off to sleep.

Once again, the letter from her father was left unopened and she had forgotten to write a letter home.

She had not thought of Guernsey at all during the day.

Villacoublay, Paris, France

With no plane to fly, Bernhard was not called to fly that night but was called in by the Oberleutnant to review the damage caused to RAF Debden from their raid early that morning. The pictures had been enlarged and the clarity was amazing. He could clearly see several bomb craters across the airfield and at least one building had been damaged.

The Oberleutnant was pleased with the results and explained that a concerted campaign of night bombing would be developed as a result. He was also told a new Heinkel 111 would be waiting for him in the morning.

After the briefing, he went back to the mess and enjoyed a schnapps with Willie and Max and shared some stories from their campaigns over Europe before they arrived here in France. They all admired the new flashes on his uniform which had now been sewn in place and toasted his promotion.

As they were thinking about getting ready for bed a dozen crews were getting ready for tonight's raid over England and they all went up to the tower to watch the planes take off, and wish them well. At 11.30pm the Oberleutnant himself fired a flare and with that the first planes taxied to the end of the runway and as had happened the previous night, took off on a runway lit by truck lights. In less than ten minutes the four Kettes of Heinkels were airborne and off on their mission.

Bernhard asked the Oberleutnant where they were headed. 'Biggin Hill,' he replied. 'It will be a tough one.'

With that they went back to the mess, toasted the crews who had just taken off with a final schnapps and headed off to bed.

Chapter 8 – Wednesday 26th June 1940

In the News

Soviet Union demands territories of Bessarabia and Northern Bukovina from Romania

Guernsey

The news Laurence and Lily were waiting for came today. The papers were full of stories about how the islanders had been welcomed in the UK and how all was well with the schools. Children seemed to be spread across the country from the North of England to Scotland. The boys of Vauvert School had even managed to send letters home to let their parents know all was well.

Meanwhile, in Guernsey, life seemed to go on as normal with 118,000 chips of tomatoes being exported. Lily in her new job picking tomatoes, had never worked so hard and the pile of paperwork seemed to grow even bigger as Laurence too felt the strain of the push to export as many tomatoes as possible before… well who know what was going to happen.

More limits were being placed on fuel, as supplies were beginning to run short. The potential for the island to secure imports when fuel generally was so vital to the war effort seemed remote.

It was also reported in the papers that not one single family had left Sark.

The fact that all was well in the United Kingdom and Rachel was there on her own made them consider their options once again.

Breakfast went down in a hurry, scrambled eggs and fried tomatoes to give them some stamina throughout the day. Lily made sandwiches for her and Laurence as they had no time to pop home for lunch. They agreed to talk about what they should do after tea that evening.

With a kiss and a hug, Laurence and Lily went their separate ways leaving Ma in charge of Laura and Michael. The children would walk back with Ma to her house and would soon be playing in her huge back garden.

At the vinery, Lily was soon happily picking tomatoes, her mind occasionally straying to a lovely night of cuddles with her gorgeous husband. She was so proud of Laurie but knew he still wished he could go and fight for his country. He was fiercely proud of being English, despite being an adopted Guernsey man, and would give anything to be able to don his uniform again and join in the fight.

Secretly she was pleased he couldn't go away and fight and dreaded the thought of losing him in the same way Ma had lost her husband. She worried though what might happen if he couldn't get off the island and had thoughts about what the Germans might do to him as an ex-soldier, if they should invade.

That lunch time, Lily sat and ate her sandwiches along with the other workers. They sat on makeshift benches made of wooden pallets. The discussion was all about the war and about family members that had already made the move to England. Lily rarely chipped in, preferring to keep her own counsel, but the discussion fascinated her and made her think more about their options.

Despite the war there was still a load of banter and of course a few jokes, some of which were a bit too risqué for Lily. She found herself blushing more than once, but was still confident enough to get everyone back to work, sharp at 12.30pm after their half hour lunch break.

Laurence decided to ride to work today and pulled his bike from the shed and gave it a quick dust to remove a few cobwebs and checked the tyres before setting off on his short journey.

He had spent some time over the previous weekend mending a puncture and lovingly polishing their only means of transport. He was pleased his puncture repair had held. Michael loved to play with the bell and had been dragged away from 'helping Dad' as the constant ringing had given Laurence a headache.

The ride was amazing, there were fewer vehicles on the roads it seemed and the sun glinted over the sea, sparkling the waters that rippled between Guernsey and the other islands. He parked the bike outside the office and sat down at his desk just as the kettle finished boiling. He tucked his sandwich into the top drawer of his desk and gladly accepted his first cup of tea of the day.

The queue of lorries was already well off the quay and heading north along the front. He knew he was in for another busy day, but he too smiled at memories of last night and looked forward to the end of the day and once more being in the arms of his lovely wife. Life was still good and he was reluctant to see that change.

Villacoublay, Paris, France

Bernhard was called in for another briefing.

This time they were told there had been a change of tactics. The Luftwaffe had decided the large daylight group attacks on England were proving too costly so daytime raids would be made in small groups. They would also vary their choice of targets to try and cause as much confusion as possible to the British defenders and the RAF.

Each pilot was called up in turn and given his target for the day. Bernhard had a mission to bomb an airfield called Kenley and with him would be one of the Dorniers. He surmised that they would be assessing which aircraft performed best at low altitude.

He also learned that a larger formation of Heinkels would take off at the same time but would circle back in mid channel to distract the enemy fighters and hopefully keep them away from his raid. It was hoped the tactic would draw out the British who could then be engaged by their own fighters. He knew the Messerschmitt 109 was the equal of the British Spitfire, and with this element of surprise he hoped this would give them the edge in battle.

Anything that helped him get back safely was good news to him.

The more he thought about it the more excited he was at this new tactic and hoped it would work well. To conclude the briefing the Oberleutnant reported on the outcome of the raid on Biggin Hill.

Apparently, all but one of the Heinkels had returned to the base safely. The one they had lost had been damaged by flak and had been seen attempting a crash landing in Kent. They all hoped the crew had been able to walk away from the landing but either way, their war was over. The report on damage caused by the raid had yet to come in but once again the night attack strategy seemed to work well.

Once the briefing was over he headed straight out to the airfield. Together with Willie they gave their replacement plane a thorough inspection and talked to the ground crew, who were just completing the fueling of the Heinkel 111. He wanted to see if there was anything they needed to know about the plane, but all seemed to be well and the new plane was in excellent condition. The mission was scheduled for noon and he hoped the British would be having their lunch and would leave them alone.

At 11.55 am precisely he was taxiing towards the end of the runway, closely followed by the rest of the *Gruppe* and a few Dorniers from Aufklarungsgruppe 123.

He and his new friend Max, the pilot of the Dornier he was partnering on the raid, took off together to the west and then circled north towards England. It seemed strange being in the air by themselves as very quickly they left all of the other aircraft behind.

As they crossed the French coast, over the Normandy beaches, they quickly descended to about 100 metres above sea level. This wasn't difficult for Bernhard as he had practised this many times during their pilot training. They turned towards the east and then headed towards the white cliffs of Dover. Together, they pulled up just enough to clear the cliff tops, disturbing flocks of sheep and a few individuals out walking.

They were spotted by coastal observers and their presence reported to fighter command but they were travelling so quickly and so low it was difficult for anyone to guess where they were heading. The German diversion was also working well and most of the south coast squadrons were being sent to hunt down the larger formations, leaving Bernhard and Max alone.

As a precaution, they headed further east towards Dartford as if they were going to attack the East London Docks but as they got within 30 miles of the city they swung around to the west and headed back towards their target, the RAF base at Kenley.

They had spotted the odd barrage balloon and the occasional shot had been fired in their direciion but nothing came close enough to cause them any concern. The countryside looked beautiful in the sunshine as they roared overhead. He could make out orchards, farmers in their fields and herds of cattle in what he knew was known as the Garden of England. The sound of his navigator in his ear brought him back into the moment.

They were on their final approach to Kenley and he gently pulled back on the stick to begin a slow climb to get a better angle for their bomb run. They were within a mile of the airport boundary at about 200 metres when a sudden flash was seen from the edge of the airport and a dozen or more smoke trails rose ahead of them. Instinctively both aircraft broke formation to avoid the smoke. Bernhard broke left and Max broke right. In the seconds before they reached the smoke trails Bernhard spotted what looked like thin string or maybe a net hanging from a row of parachutes.

While he had just managed to avoid the strings, Max's Dornier hadn't been as lucky. The breeze was blowing the parachutes to the right and the last in the line snagged around the left wing of the Dornier.

He swung back to the right and could see Max struggling with the controls as the string had a parachute at the bottom end too. He seemed to get his machine under control and was soon heading back towards the south. In the split seconds that had passed he was now over the runway and a shout from Willie brought him back to the job in hand.

Without further thought he pulled the bomb release lever and pushed the Heinkel at full speed away from Kenley and the new weapon. A few of the guns that protected the airport helped chase him away as he turned south on a similar route to Max to see if he could spot the Dornier or perhaps help him get back. His keen eyes soon spotted Max and his crew, still trailing a long wire with a torn parachute at the end. One of his gunners reported that his bombs had landed on the airport but had missed the main runway but that was the last thing on his mind at that moment.

As he flew low across the English countryside he thought about all of the people who lived in the houses below him and how, like his parents, they were having to cope with the war. People were making decisions every day as to how to survive the turmoil, others, through no fault of their own were suffering and dying because of decisions being made by the leaders of their country.

Some of those people in their nice country houses had sons like him, fighting in foreign fields for reasons that were largely forgotten. Why were they doing this? Why was he trying to kill people? Why were people he didn't even know trying to kill him?

His reverie was shattered as a wall of barrage balloons appeared ahead of him. They found themselves close to the well defended port of Dover. He veered to starboard and, with Max following close by, they steered well clear of the coastal anti-aircraft guns which surrounded the port, and headed out across the channel. He breathed a sigh of relief as he left English soil behind him and set a course for Paris.

After a successful landing, and another round of applause from the crew, he crawled out of his aircraft and walked quickly across to debriefing. It was there that he listened to Max's story and heard for himself exactly what weapon he had just seen.

Apparently, they had witnessed a parachute and cable defence system which fired rockets into the air in front of the attacking aircraft. Each rocket dragged a wire, like a piano wire behind it and was designed to cut into the wing of an aircraft. Once snagged the parachutes would then cause so much drag on the aircraft it would cause it to crash.

After the debriefing Max took him across to see the damage for himself. Luckily for Max the parachutes had been damaged and didn't cause the intended drag but a deep cut had been made into his port wing and a long length of wire was being carefully removed by the ground crew. One engineer had already suffered a nasty cut trying to pull the wire out of the wing.

Several reports had been filed about this system, but as yet, no aircraft had been reported lost.

Something else to worry about, Bernhard thought!

Magloch House, Scotland

Over a breakfast of eggs and bacon, Rachel had asked Mary about piano lessons and she had agreed to see if that could be arranged. Today they would be taught how to sew. The Mistress of the house had asked Mary to do what she could to "educate" the girls in the arts that women needed to become successful housewives.

They would be shown how to cook, knit and grow vegetables. They would also be required to keep their room and their bathroom tidy and one of the cleaning staff would show them how to do that properly.

Later in the morning they were sitting around the big table in the kitchen with their instructor, a dressmaker who apparently made all the fine clothes and dresses for the lady of the house. They were making a simple apron which they would be able to use in the kitchen when Cook showed them how to cook. Rachel seemed to take to it like a duck to water and was engrossed in making her blue apron, when a loud screeching noise made her jump and prick her finger with the needle.

She jumped up with a yelp and the other two girls almost fell off their chairs as the awful noise suddenly turned into a rather nice sound. From the boot room near the back door came Young Jack blowing into an instrument none of the girls had ever seen before. Mary laughed at their reaction and was soon dancing around the table, clapping her hands in time with the music.

The dressmaker seemed quite upset at the interruption and started waving her arms around to stop Young Jack from playing.

'Will you hush those bagpipes,' she yelled above the din.

Young Jack ignored her but seeing the angry look on her face, he smiled at the girls between breaths, winked at Mary then turned on his heels and marched off down the corridor towards the back door.

'Well, whatever next,' the dressmaker muttered. 'Come on girls back to your aprons.'

Mary saw Rachel sucking her finger and took her across to the tap, running cold water over the pinprick and then wrapped a handkerchief around her finger and held it tight until the blood stopped running.

'Fingers heal quickly,' she told Rachel and once again Rachel couldn't help but smile in response to Mary's lovely smile.

As they stood there Rachel asked her about the bagpipes. Mary explained it was a Scottish instrument and was played at all of the great Scottish events and especially at midnight at the end of the year to welcome in the New Year. Rachel thought she would like to hear that and wondered if they would still be there by the end of the year.

That made her think of Christmas at home with her family and she suddenly realised, with a flush of guilt, that she hadn't thought of home for a few days and had forgotten to write her letter.

She asked Mary if she would find her a pen and paper so she could write a letter to her parents. Mary promised to help her that afternoon, after the aprons were finished and they had eaten their lunch.

Soon she was back at the table working away on her apron and for the first time in a while she had tears in her eyes as she thought of home and her mum and dad. Most of all she felt sick inside that she had not yet sent them a letter to tell them where she was and that she was safe.

How could she be so selfish, she thought to herself.

Guernsey

After an exhausting day at work, both Laurence and Lily had been glad to get home and after a quick supper of cheese and biscuits they sat deep in their own thoughts for some time while a record played in the background.

The children were playing in the back yard.

A gentle breeze rattled the windows as if the wind was echoing the distant sound of guns, except there weren't any. Europe was now dominated by Germany and across the water in France and across most of Europe, all was relatively quiet as populations got used to German occupation and right now there was little organised resistance.

But the war was still threatening to do what they believed nothing could ever do - tear them apart.

After the children had gone to bed they spoke about the possibility of Lily and the children leaving the island. Many cups of tea were drunk as they considered their options.

There seemed to be three potential routes ahead.

They could stay together on the island and hope the Germans wouldn't invade, they would probably be cut off from Britain and Rachel, and as the war progressed a shortage of food could become a problem.

Alternatively, they could stay in Guernsey under German occupation, if they came, and that held potential risks to Lily and the children, or they could leave Laurence and head off to goodness knows where in the UK and try and get to Rachel.

Little thought was given to how long they might be apart but by the end of the evening, before they finally went to bed, the subject was raised.

Laurence felt he knew something of war having been in the army, and he had been amazed at the speed of the German *Blitzkrieg*. He felt the German progress seemed impossible to stop and they had to believe that if they did invade England they could well succeed. His only cause for hope was the strength of the British navy and the hope that they would stop any invasion force. If Hitler did invade England he felt the islands might be by-passed but would fall under German rule eventually.

Could England be defended and could Mr. Churchill stir the nation into an heroic defence?

No-one could tell. Suffice to say if they left the island they may never come back.

Whatever happens they concluded they would do all they could to stay together.

At 9.35pm they turned the radio on and listened to Rhythm on Reeds on the Home Service as a distraction. At 10 o'clock Henry Hall's Guest Night came on but they didn't bother to listen to the whole show and after checking all was secure and all lights were out, they headed up to bed.

As they were getting ready for bed, Lily went to the window and looked out across the sea towards France, the sea glistened in the moonlight and she looked up at the crescent moon, thinking how beautiful the world could be. She said a silent prayer for Rachel to be OK and then climbed into bed.

Lily smiled and nestled herself alongside her husband. Feeling safe once again, she quickly fell asleep. Laurence lay there for a while deep in thought. The decision had been made, but could that really happen. The only way they could achieve that would be for them to stay in Guernsey. Laurence knew in his heart there would come a point when Lily would have to take the children to England and he would have to stay. He knew that once the Germans arrived there would be little chance of leaving the island.

He would have to find a way to get away and the sooner the better.
He eventually fell asleep and had a restless night dreaming of German soldiers, German planes and columns of refugees with his family amongst them, just like he had seen on the news reels at the North Cinema on Monday night.

Magloch House, Scotland

After supper, Rachel went to her room to write her letter home. As she sat on her bed she noticed the letter, which was now propped up on the cupboard, no doubt by the considerate Mary.

She opened it and read her father's words, bursting into tears as soon as she started. *How could she have forgotten them so easily*, she thought. She then realized how hard it must have been for them to have made the decision to send her away, which ultimately led to her being safe from the war and living in luxury here in Scotland.

She hid the precious pound note her Dad had given her in the top draw of her cupboard and, with a heavy heart, she sat down to write her letter home.

Dear Mum and Dad, Laura and Michael

I am safe here in Scotland, living in a big house in the country called Magloch House. I have been riding horses, rowed on a lake, fished for trout and am learning to sew and cook. I have Christine and Julie with me and we are having a lovely time.

We all sleep in a big room and we have a nice lady called Mary to look after us.

Dad, have you ever heard bagpipes, they are amazing!!

I hope you can all come up here sometime to live with us, that would be just great.

I miss you all so much and hope we can see each other soon.

With all my Love

Rachel xxx

When Mary popped into the bedroom to tuck them all in, Rachel asked her if she would arrange to have the letter sent to her home in Guernsey. She showed Mary the letter from her Father, which had their home address on it, and Mary agreed that they would go together in the carriage the next day to the local village to get a stamp and post it.

After lights out and the other girls were asleep, Rachel got out of bed and looked up at the moon. She wondered if her Mum was looking at the moon too and a few silent tears crept down her face. She climbed quietly back into bed and whispered a little prayer, that her family would be kept safe and well and that they would all be back together soon.

Villacoublay, Paris, France

Bernhard enjoyed a restful late afternoon and early evening, during which he had slept in the sun for at least an hour in his deckchair, with Greif at his feet. He eventually headed off to the mess for some food before the evening briefing.

He expected to be back in the air that night and it would be interesting to see where they were headed this time.

At 9pm sharp he was sitting next to Willie in the briefing room waiting for the curtain to be drawn back.

Before they started, Max was asked to talk to the group about the weapon they had encountered. He gave them a graphic description of the rocket based system and the Oberleutnant asked Bernhard if he had anything to add, but Max had spoken so well he couldn't offer any more information.

After Max had sat back down, the Oberleutnant pulled back the curtain and the map of the south of England was revealed. This time the pins and ribbons guided them towards Wales and the route ended up over the docks in Swansea. He would be attacking with just his Kette of three planes while others would be attacking targets along the way. They would be taking off in stages and Bernhard's Kette would be going first as they had the furthest distance to travel.

Bernhard went back to his billet and set his faithful alarm for 10.55pm and tried to get some sleep but his siesta that afternoon had taken the edge off his tiredness and he lay awake for an hour waiting for his alarm to go off. In his mind, he tried to envisage life back in Germany. It seemed like many years since he had been home but in truth it had been around 3 months since he had spent a week at home with his parents.

He had been born and raised in Dresden, a beautiful city which sat on the River Elbe. He hoped the war was far enough away from his home and that his parents and sister would be safe from all of the hardships much of Europe was facing.

As he lay there he thought of the walks they used to take along the river banks and into the woods and how he and his sister Greta played with Wolf, their dog, throwing sticks for him to fetch. They used to spend many happy hours chasing each other through the trees and playing with their dog.

Would they ever be together like that again? he wondered.

He made a note to write another letter home tomorrow. A nagging thought that putting off writing the letter until after the raid may not be a good idea, was quickly dismissed. He had no time for negative thoughts. If nothing else he was confident in his abilities and those of his crew and the thought that they wouldn't make it home was a rare thought indeed.

Unable to sleep, he got up and focused his mind back on the task in hand. He was dressed and about to leave his room when the alarm went off. He walked down the corridor, knocking on Willie's door on the way. He came straight out and together they walked out into the night to undertake their next mission.

As usual he kicked the tyres and once everyone else was on board, climbed in to do some system checks and make sure all was ready for the flight. The fuel tanks were full and the 8 bombs they were carrying sat, nose upwards in their cradles. All of the guns were fully armed and he spoke to each of the 3 K's in turn before he sat down and was ready to go.

At 11.50pm he fired up the engines in response to a flashlight signal from the tower. Along with the other two planes in his Kette he made his way to the end of the runway. The sky was relatively clear with some broken cloud and the moonlight made maneuvering easy. As on previous missions they would be met by a night fighter escort and they would lead the

Heinkels part of the way to the target and would also give them some protection in case RAF night fighters tried to attack them.

As his watch hit midnight the flare went up and a row of truck lights came on to guide him down the runway.

They were off.

Chapter 9 – Thursday 27th June 1940

In the News

German Forces complete occupation of France by reaching Spain
Britain announces a blockade of the European coast from the Bay of Biscay to the north of Norway
French Battleship Jean Bart escapes from St Nazaire
The Germans start using the Enigma Machine

Villacoublay, Paris, France

The flare had barely gone out when Bernhard and his crew took off and headed west. He had taken off shortly after midnight and was soon leading his Kette of three Heinkels from Kampfgeschwader 55 out over the Channel.

The moon was bright and he could see the coast of England clearly, although not a light was in sight. He led the aircraft almost as far as Exeter before heading north towards Exmoor to the west of Taunton.

Their night fighter escort had turned back as they approached Exeter.

The plan was that two more fighters would be waiting for them in this same area as they made their journey home.

From Taunton, they crossed the Bristol Channel and headed to the west of Swansea. As they crossed the coast they turned north east and lined up on Swansea Docks. They had been following a pathfinder, night equipped, Dornier and as they flew over the docks the Dornier dropped a large flare which lit up the target for Bernhard's Kette of three aircraft. Flying right over the illuminated target Bernhard dropped his bombs on a signal from Willie and immediately turned south and headed back across the south west of England towards the channel.

They had been unopposed throughout their flight.

One of his gunners reported seeing explosions in the harbour area, but once again they would have to wait until the next day before they would find out how successful their mission had been. The night fighter escorts picked them up off the coast near Exeter and they flew back in formation until they approached Paris. The lead escort flicked his lights as they peeled away.

It had been the perfect mission.

They landed before 5am as the sky was brightening and were soon taxiing across to their stand. Paris had looked amazing in the early morning light and life seemed good to Bernhard and his crew who had applauded loudly once again as their wheels touched the concrete.

They were soon walking across the runway to a debriefing which was followed by a hearty breakfast. The crew all sat at the same table and the discussion was all about the raid and what damage they might have caused. After about an hour Bernhard headed back to his room to catch up on some well-earned rest. He was asleep within seconds of his head hitting the pillow.

Guernsey

Laurence woke in a sweat. His dream had culminated with German Stuka dive bombers attacking the column of refugees and amongst them were Lily and the children. They had been running from the bombs and the children had been crying out for their Daddy as they had disappeared into a cloud of smoke and debris.

The dream gave him a feeling of dread and he wanted to tell Lily how worried he was.

He turned over to discover he was alone in the bed. He sat up with a start and looked around the room. Lily was sitting in the window watching the sun rise over the neighbouring island of Herm. He sensed she was crying and immediately got out of bed to comfort her.

'When the war is over, do you think we will be here, in our lovely home, all happy together?'

He put his arm around her, turned her face to his and kissed the tears from her cheeks.

'Of course, my love. One day we will all be here together again,' he replied. 'Maybe for Christmas,' he added hopefully.

He decided not to tell her about his dreams.

Lily turned back to the wonderful display that nature was providing.

The war seemed a million miles away but Laurence decided that when he got to work he would get tickets, to enable Lily and the children to leave the island.

He realized that if they did leave, things might never be the same again, but of all the options it seemed the best for his precious family.

Breakfast was the usual mad rush with Michael doing his best not to cooperate as always. Lily made cheese and tomato sandwiches for her and Laurence and Ma arrived at her usual time to help get the children ready for the day. Ma noticed that Lily was a little red eyed but didn't say anything while everyone was so busy.

As soon as the breakfast dishes were washed and put away, Ma took Laura and Michael home with her to play in her garden.

As they walked away, Lily watched from the front door and smiled as Michael, so full of energy, was almost pulling his Grandmothers arm off as he tried to run up the road.

Meanwhile Laurence, snuck up behind her and putting his arms around her waist, kissed the back of her head, whispered 'I love you' in her ear and then crossed the road to catch the bus into work. Lily waved to them all and then went back inside to hang her apron up. She washed her hands, splashed her face to cool down, checked everything was tidy and then headed off to the greenhouses. It was 7.30am.

Laurence's bus was on time when it reached the halfway, but it was standing room only. From his position on the bus he could see out of the window towards Herm. A group of fishing boats were heading out to sea and a larger vessel headed north. Laurence pondered if she was carrying more evacuees. Once he climbed off the bus opposite the Royal Hotel, he walked to his office, past the long row of tomato trucks already waiting to be unloaded.

As he sat down, Agnes brought him a steaming cup of tea and he sat back and took a moment to say thank you and enjoy the taste before settling into his day.

The stack of paperwork seemed higher than ever, mirroring the growing number of trucks waiting to unload. During the morning, he popped out to the passenger desk and reserved three, free open tickets to England for Lily and the children. He asked if he could buy a ticket for himself but was told places on the boats were only available for women, children and men of military age. He had known the answer but thought he would ask anyway.

The time flew by but just before lunchtime he felt the need to stretch his legs and took a walk along the pier to talk to some of the drivers as they waited to be unloaded.

It was during a discussion, about the fast spreading rumour that the States were taking over control of all the greenhouses and how that might affect wages, that they heard the telltale sound of an aircraft passing over head.

He and several of the drivers strained their eyes, looking into the summer sun and soon fingers were pointing towards a solitary plane that was circling slowly over St Peter Port.

The watchers soon lost interest as it was too high to see whether it was friend or foe and it didn't seem a threat. He went back to the office and tucked into his cheese sandwiches. He was also happy to see a nice green apple and a few strawberries tucked in with his sandwich, and pictured Lily sneaking the treat into his bag. He could only imagine how much she would have enjoyed doing that, knowing he would appreciate the luxury of fresh fruit with his lunch.

His mood changed as he tried to imagine how he could survive without her. Being away from her for nearly 12 hours a day was bad enough, but when should they go? The time would never be right.

The news reports were just getting worse and he had started to believe the Nazis would invade soon. He couldn't see Hitler ignoring the chance to capture a piece of British territory, despite it being so small and undefended.

Suddenly there was a commotion outside and he ran to the window just in time to see a German Dornier aircraft come from the direction of Salerie Corner and roar across the harbour, a few hundred feet above the cranes and disappear to the south. People were huddling together in conversation and he was suddenly aware that Agnes, the office secretary, was standing next to him.

'What will become of us?' She asked absentmindedly.

'Who knows,' he replied. He understood why she might be worried. She was young and single and if the Germans came no-one knew how they might treat her.

'I am sure they won't come here,' he added, trying to calm her nerves. 'We have been demilitarised and the islands are of no real use to the Germans. They'll probably leave us alone.'

He tried to sound confident and smiled at her as they stood there.

'Let's have a cup of tea,' she said, seeming suddenly happier. He was sure she was just being brave.

A cup of tea soon appeared on his desk and work became the usual distraction and the afternoon flew by in a flurry of paperwork. He picked up the paper as usual before getting the bus home. The headlines confirmed the rumour that the States were taking over the abandoned farms and greenhouses and more jobs were available for all those able to work.

Money would be the least of our worries, he thought.

One worrying story was that of a young girl who had been evacuated and who had died upon arrival in the UK. It seemed she had been ill before they left so maybe the stress of the journey had been the cause. He read the sad news and felt for her family. Of course, it brought thoughts of Rachel and how she was getting on in England.

Not knowing the answer brought tears to his eyes as the bus made its way along the front to their house.

He tried to focus on the booking the band had for the dance at the Royal Hotel that night. He was looking forward to making some music and seeing everyone dancing along. Music always lifted his spirits.

Villacoublay, Paris, France

Max, Bernhard's friend, and one of the Dornier pilots from Aufklarungsgruppe 12, had been given, what he considered, an easy day. The morning briefing had been quick as he had been designated a mission to carry out reconnaissance over the Channel Islands.

They had taken off in ideal conditions at around 10.30am and quickly climbed to 3,000 metres above the Bay of St Malo. From there he could see all of the Channel Islands laid out below them from Alderney in the north to Jersey in the south.

Just before noon he had circled over Guernsey and his cameraman was busy taking photos, at the same time that Laurence was looking at him from the harbour. Max was anxious not to stay too long over the islands. He was convinced they had no anti-aircraft defence, so that wasn't a concern, but there was always the chance of being ambushed by a roaming fighter while his attention was focused on getting into position to take a good set of photographs.

Soon his observer gave him the thumbs up and he turned to the north before diving down to 300 metres for a quick pass across the islands. That way he would get a closer look at what was happening in the ports. He turned and came in towards Guernsey, crossing the island from L'Ancresse in the north, skimming over the parishes of the Vale and St Sampsons, before heading across the harbour of St Peter Port.

From there he skimmed over the quiet seas to the north of Jersey then crossed that island, passing low over St Helier, and then headed out to sea towards the French coast just south of Portbail. Flying across the French countryside the war seemed a world away. He flew south of Caen and then dropped towards the south of Paris, circling the airport to land into the gentle westerly breeze.

The photos were developed quickly on base and during the debriefing they could all clearly see the queues of trucks lined up at the Harbour in Guernsey and several boats being loaded with cargo. Max confirmed that the trucks were all heavily loaded and many were painted green like army trucks. The report was passed up the line and everyone waited for fresh orders.

Max found a deckchair next to Bernhard who was half asleep with his faithful dog lying by his side. He told Bernhard about his flight and what he had seen from the pictures.

Bernhard was suddenly wide awake. He had a bad feeling about the news. He had a soft spot for Guernsey and was hoping it would be bypassed by the war. He tried to put his worries to one side.

'Those trucks?' he asked. 'Do you think they really were army?'

'Not sure.' Max replied. 'Some of them certainly looked military and I could see men in brown overalls or uniforms?'

Bernhard couldn't believe that they were military. No-one had fired a shot and he had heard that all military personnel had left the island a while ago.

He settled down again and the warmth of the sun soon took away the chill of concern he had felt.

If only all days were like this, he thought as he lay in the sun. *This was how a war should be fought.*

Magloch House, Scotland

Today the girls were being shown how to cook.

They had started by helping Cook with the breakfast and were now making bread ready for lunch. Mary had arranged with Young Jack that the carriage would be ready after lunch and it was agreed Mary and Rachel would drive to the Post Office while he took Julie and Christine out on the lake fishing.

Rachel's bread wasn't very good and she knew her Mum would be disappointed in her efforts, as she was such a great baker. Cook reassured her and told her she would get better as she got bigger.

'You don't have the strength you need to knead the dough properly young Lassie,' Cook told her in her soft Scottish lilt.

After they had eaten a cheese sandwich at lunch time, Mary and Rachel headed off in the carriage for the village. Cook called after them telling them not to be late as she wanted to show Rachel how to cook a roast.

They clip clopped along the country lanes with Jock happily pulling them along. Occasionally he would be distracted by something particularly tasty to eat growing on the hedges, but a quick flick of the reins and he would regain his momentum and carry on down the narrow lane.

As they travelled along in the peace and quiet of the Scottish countryside Mary, for the first time, started to ask Rachel about home.

Rachel happily spoke of her parents and her siblings, their small home in Guernsey and about the island itself. She promised Mary that she could come and visit them after the war was over. That caused several minutes of silence as both had their private thoughts about what that meant and when that might happen. In truth, you could not feel further from the war in that carriage, in that quiet country lane, in the heart of Scotland.

They soon arrived in the small village and Mary tied Jock to a ring in the wall of the local pub then walked with Rachel to the Post Office, which was situated next door. They bought a stamp with the money Rachel's father had given her, and they left the envelope with the Post Mistress to start its journey to Guernsey.

Mary took Rachel on a short walk around the village. It was a picture postcard scene with a small church, or Kirk as Mary called it, a smithy, complete with the sound of metal being worked, and a variety of cute stone cottages, many sporting beautiful roses climbing their walls.

A stream ran through the village and into a large pond, several ducks and a pair of swans were swimming about. They were the first swans Rachel had ever seen.

The pub was called the Magloch Inn and had letting rooms for visitors to stay in. Mary offered Rachel the chance to pop in and see what it was like. She had never been in a pub before, so a little nervously, she agreed to go in and have a look around.

Mary held her hand and took Rachel into the bar. The place was virtually empty with just two old villagers sitting in the corner playing dominoes and putting the world to rights as men the world over were inclined to do when they had a drink in their hands.

Mary knew the land lady who was drying glasses behind the bar. Her name was Norma Bateman. She asked for two lemonades and while they were being poured the girls went and sat in a corner table. Norma brought them over and smiled.

'There you go girlies,' she said and winked at Rachel before heading back to her place behind the bar.

Rachel looked around, fascinated by this new experience.

There was a large fireplace with a huge fish in a glass case above it. The fish was a pike, Mary explained. There were photos of anglers with their catches on all of the walls and lots of horse brasses, together with old fishing rods and reels. The smell of the fire, even though it wasn't lit, was strong and Rachel imagined how cozy and friendly it would be in the evenings, when the fire was lit and it was cold outside.

Once they had finished their lemonades and Mary had paid Norma, they went back to Jock, took the hay bag off his head which Mary had put on when they had arrived, and untied him. They walked him across to a water trough so he could have a drink and then climbed back on to the carriage and headed back to "the big house", as Mary called it, so Rachel could help make the roast.

It was a beautiful day and the countryside looked amazing as they headed home.

Rachel and Mary hardly spoke on the way back. When Mary glanced at Rachel she noticed she seemed to have a permanent smile etched on her face. Mary smiled to herself, she looked at Rachel again and thought this was one happy little girl who had left her troubles far behind.

Villacoublay, Paris, France

Bernhard's afternoon reverie was broken when the Oberleutnant summoned them all for another briefing.

Where to next, he thought as they headed into the large briefing room.

This time the map revealed several targets on the east coast of England and the sheer number of pins and strings indicated a highly-coordinated raid with bombers from several bases joining in the attack. Bernhard followed the strings from Villacoublay and could see their target was Sunderland, a major port in the North East of England. The route was out into the North Sea and then they would be using the tried and tested night fighter escort and *Knickebein* beam system to put them over the target. Other bombers would be joining the raid from Norway.

The main target was the docks but they also had a secondary target of RAF Usworth, located near Sunderland. The weather forecast looked good and the plan was to bomb the target from 3,000 metres.

Bernhard had quickly worked out that this was the farthest they would have travelled on a mission and that it would take over two hours there and two hours back. It was probably as far as they could go with a full bomb load and a full fuel load. The good news though was that for most of the journey they would be over the North Sea and as such should be safe from British night fighters.

Take off was scheduled for 9pm so after the briefing he and Willie took a stroll around the airport perimeter to discuss the raid.

Bernhard had every faith in his friend and navigator and as they spoke he felt confident that this would be another easy mission for him and the rest of the crews of Kampfgeschwader 55. There were still a couple of hours to go before they were called so they headed back to the crew's mess.

While some crews liked a drink before they flew, Bernhard insisted all of his crew were stone cold sober before they took off. They played cards for a while, then Bernhard headed back to his room for an hour's sleep before roll call at 8pm. He tried to sleep but didn't feel tired at all so got out his maps and looked up Sunderland, a place he had never heard of, and did some research.

He saw that the docks were extensive and ship building was a big industry. There were also areas of coal mining close by and RAF Usworth was based just to the south of the city. He saw that the lighthouse at Roker would be a good marker, but of course during the war it would be turned off. If there was enough light from the moon he hoped the distinctive shape of the piers would stand out and lead them straight to the target.

This was a far riskier target than Swansea the night before so he picked up a pen and paper and wrote a short letter to his sister in Dresden.

He told her how well he was, about his dog and gave her some general information about Paris and suggested they could all meet up in the Champs Elysees after the war was over. He popped the letter into an envelope and addressed it and left it on his bedside table.

He knew if he didn't get back someone would send it to his sister for him.

Magloch House, Scotland

Rachel had spent the rest of her afternoon preparing vegetables with her friends, under the watchful eye of Cook. She had watched as a large lump of beef had been placed in the oven on a low heat for two hours of cooking. The smell in the kitchen was heavenly and all of the girls felt their mouths watering in anticipation of the feast to come.

The food was also being prepared for the owners of the house and a small number of guests who were visiting tonight so Cook was making sure everything was just right.

The dinner party wasn't scheduled until 7pm so the girls and staff would eat their food first and the staff jokingly said the guests would get the leftovers.

The supper was amazing and the gravy, made with the juices from the beef and the water from the vegetables was just heavenly. Well so Rachel thought.

'Almost as good as my Mum's,' she whispered to Mary so Cook couldn't hear.

As they cleared away their tea, the first course was delivered to the dinner party and then Cook announced that they would be needed to help with the main course.

Each girl was given a tureen of vegetables to serve to the dinner table. The three Blue and White china tureens were filled with roast potatoes, carrots and cabbage respectively and then in a procession, following Cook, they walked into the main dining room and were told to place the tureens on the table between the guests.

Rachel was nervous, as were the others, and she was worried she might drop her tureen.

Thankfully, they all found their way safely on to the large table. Cook asked the girls to line up and she explained to the dinner party that all of the girls had helped to prepare the food. The Lady of the house smiled at the girls and whispered, 'well done.' Then Cook led them back out of the room.

As soon as the door shut behind them the girls erupted into a frenzied conversation about how amazing that experience had been and how beautiful all of the women were and how handsome the men were in their dinner jackets and bow ties.

They were still excited as they made their way to their bedroom and Rachel couldn't help but look down into the dining room as they walked along the balcony. The meal was all but over now and the men stood in a corner smoking cigars and drinking whisky while the women had grouped around the end of the table and were also in deep conversation. Rachel wondered if they were talking about them but dismissed the idea.

We are not that important, she thought as they walked on to their room. *I suppose they have a lot more important things to talk about.*

It wasn't long before she was washed and tucked up in her bed. She pictured her Mum getting her letter and how happy it would make her and maybe how sad it would make her too. She wondered what was happening in Guernsey as she drifted off to sleep. Her dreams were full of horses and food as she enjoyed a trouble free 9 hours of sleep.

Villacoublay, Paris, France

As always Bernhard had been waiting for roll call and was one of the first to the final briefing before takeoff. The weather report was good but there was a chance of low cloud so they would need to rely on the *Knickebein* beam system and their night fighter escorts. They would also meet up with several Kettes of Heinkels from Luftflotte 5 based in Oslo. If everything went to plan they would arrive over Sunderland at 11.30pm.

At 8.30pm as the sun started to set Bernhard and his crew went out to the plane, Bernhard did his usual tour of inspection and kicked the tyres before being the last to climb on board. There would be no need for any runway lights this evening as the clear sky ensured it would still be light long after they had taken off.

Kampfgeschwader 55 had mustered 42 aircraft for the raid, one of the biggest *Gruppe* efforts yet and the hope was that the British would never suspect that their flight plan would result in an attack on the North East. The *Gruppe* took off to the west and angled sharply north, heading towards Dunkirk and the

Belgian border. Their route took them away from England heading out over the North Sea.

As they crossed Dunkirk they had climbed to 3,000 metres and were met by their night fighter escort. In the gathering gloom, they continued their journey north east. Shortly after they crossed the coast one of the planes developed a fault and with just one engine running turned back for home.

One of the lucky ones, Bernhard thought as he watched the plane peel away.

Just under halfway through the flight the night fighter escort turned back as they had reached their maximum range. They were on their own from here on in.

The Heinkel 111 was a noisy aircraft and there was little opportunity for chatting as they continued on through the night. It seemed they had been flying forever when suddenly Willie let him know they had acquired one of the beams and they should be turning west soon and heading towards the target. As the moon was still quite bright and the sky was clear they could clearly see the *Gruppe* leader bank sharply to port with his *Kette* and Bernhard and the rest of the group followed suit.

Below them what looked like a grey mist was gathering and Bernhard quickly realised there would be no visual references for the attack. The low cloud was obviously over the land and was spreading out over the sea. It looked like the type of mist you would see across a field first thing in the morning or last thing at night. They had been flying in clear skies right down to sea level until now.

As they got closer Willie came forward and told him to watch the leader and take his queue for the bomb release in the next couple of minutes.

He had acquired the signal and the target was very close. Almost as the words came out of his mouth he saw a stack of bombs leaving the lead planes and he reached up for the bomb release lever and added his 8 bombs to the devastation that was falling on Sunderland from above.

As soon as the bombs were released they banked left. He could see the rest of the *Gruppe* following them and in the distance, he thought he could make out more planes coming in from the east which he thought would be the planes from *Luftflotte 5* based in Oslo.

Willie reported that they could see explosions lighting up the low clouds so something had been hit. Light flak also appeared but the ground crews were firing blind and only the planes of *Luftflotte 5* would have to worry about that.

It would be good to see the results of the raid once the reconnaissance photos came in, he thought.

Willie gave him the thumbs up and headed back to his navigation equipment and soon they were out over the clear waters of the North Sea. Not a shot had been fired at them and they had seen no enemy aircraft.

As they approached the Kent coast and the straights of Dover they experienced a brief amount of flak.

Suddenly out of the blue a Bristol Blenheim shot across the front of his plane, not more than 50 metres away. The shock made him instantly pull back on the stick and for a moment he was worried he would crash into another member of their *gruppe*. The fighter had appeared out of nowhere and he was convinced they hadn't seen his plane as it dived on another Heinkel below and to his right.

Bright flashes of cannon fire lit the sky and soon the night fighters prey was in flames and banking away to towards the sea below. In the moonlight, he could see a few parachutes appear but it was impossible to tell if everyone had bailed out safely. Their own night fighter escorts went off in pursuit of the Bristol Blenheim and then as suddenly as it had happened the skies were clear again.

Despite the noise of their engines he could still hear his heart thumping in his chest as he tried to calm his nerves after the shock of that near miss. Thankfully that was the last action they saw on this mission.

As they flew across the coast of France, Bernhard was aware of how little fuel they had left and kept an anxious watch on the fuel gauges. He had never seen the dials so low but thankfully they got back without any problems and landed to the usual round of applause on a runway lit by truck headlights. Debriefing was a quick affair as they had little to report and it was 2am in the morning.

They were sent off to get some sleep and told to be ready for another important mission the following morning.

Guernsey

Tea had been a quiet affair, eggs sausages and grilled tomatoes, which seemed to accompany every meal now.

Laurence had put on his dinner jacket and after Lily had straightened his tie he left his family to go to the dance, giving them all a kiss on the head before he left. He put on his cycle clips and pushed his bike across the road before climbing on and heading off along the front to the Royal Hotel. It was a short journey of around a mile and a half from their house and took him about ten minutes.

Lily had spent the evening playing with the children before they had gone to bed at 9pm.

Laurence wouldn't be home until around 10.30pm so she busied herself tidying the house. She hated it when she was left alone and secretly wished the closure of the dance halls had been extended.

At the Royal Hotel the dance had been lively but not as busy as usual. Laurence put that down to so many people being evacuated. Those that were there seemed intent on enjoying every minute. Glenn Miller songs had been popular and at 9.50pm they had gone into their rendition of Moonlight Serenade and repeated it as an encore before the show ended at 10pm exactly.

This was so everyone could leave before the lights out curfew.

Once they had packed their kit away Laurence picked up his bike and headed home along the front.

Lily was sitting on the sofa with the radio on when she heard Laurence come home.

He took his jacket off while Lily put the kettle on and then they snuggled on the sofa.

'You smell of smoke again my love,' Lily said wrinkling her little nose.

'Sorry,' he apologized. 'I have something to tell you.'

Lily looked at him, curious to know what was so important.

'I picked up three open tickets to England for you and the children today,' he announced. 'Just in case.'

Lily pulled back and looked at him. 'I can't go without you,' she replied. 'We have to stick together.'

'You know that won't be possible,' he replied. 'I am too old to go so they would only take you and the children.'

'This will only be as a last resort Lily,' he tried to reassure her. 'Just in case something bad happens. And you can be sure I will do whatever I can to stay with you.'

Lily sipped her tea thoughtfully. 'You think the Germans are coming, don't you?' she questioned.

'Yes, I do, I can't see Hitler missing the chance to capture a piece of British soil,' he replied. 'We are an easy target and undefended, I think it is bound to happen.'

'When do you think, they will come?' Lily asked.

'Soon my dear,' he replied. 'Very soon.'

'I think you should pack some things so you are ready to go at very short notice.'

He told her about the planes flying over the island and how he had concluded they were spying on the island to make plans for the invasion. He pictured boat loads of Germans arriving in the harbour and walking ashore unopposed.

She squeezed in closer to Laurence and held his arm. Lily's mind was racing. What would they do? Where would they go? What if Laurence couldn't get off the island and the Germans took him away?

They talked until 11.30pm and then headed off to bed, but not before Laurence got a case down from the attic and he had seen to it that Lily had packed some clothes and bits and pieces for her and the children. They also shared out what money they had so Lily wouldn't be penniless if she had to leave quickly.

Before bed he took off his dinner jacket and laid it out on Rachel's bed to air, ready for their next performance on Saturday. He hadn't told Lily about that one yet.

Chapter 10 – Friday 28th June 1940

In the News

Roosevelt signs Smith Act to register all non-US Citizens

Guernsey

The day dawned a little cloudier than of late but it would soon clear. Laurence had gone to work as usual and Lily had gone off to pick more tomatoes leaving the children with Ma.

The papers reported that some tomato crops were to be replaced with food crops to help sustain the people of Guernsey and the remaining Guernsey cattle.

Self-sufficiency in the current situation was going to be vital.

Maybe Lily wouldn't be picking tomatoes for much longer, he thought.

Laurence also noted that people could scrump food from their neighbours gardens, if they knew the owners had been evacuated, and if they had obtained a letter of authority to gain access.

He immediately had a garden in mind, it was behind one of the houses Lily used to clean. She had always said they had some wonderful fruit growing in their garden.

In the middle of the day a single Dorner 17 had been seen flying high around the island. The islanders didn't know what it was doing but it had been noted that it seemed to be on a mission to observe the island because of the way it circled above Guernsey for a while before heading east towards Jersey.

Villacoublay, Paris, France

The single Dornier 17F from Aufklarungsgruppe 123 landed at
about 2pm that afternoon. The pilot and the observer reported
immediately on their observations, which confirmed those of
Max the day before.

Reports were made, orders were given.

At around 4.30pm, Bernhard and the rest of his *Gruppe* were
called in for an emergency briefing. To his horror, he realized,
as soon as he saw the charts on the wall that one of the targets
was Guernsey in the Channel Islands. Jersey was also to be
targeted.

By 5pm the 9 aircraft were lined up on the runway with
engines roaring, waiting for the flare to go up. The
Oberleutnant was on the balcony of the airport's tower and at
5.05pm exactly he fired the flare and the first of the Heinkels
was off down the runway.

Within a few minutes his Kette of three aircraft and the other
six Heinkels were in the air and heading west across
Normandie towards Alderney.

His mission was to attack a convoy of troop trucks which had
been seen parked on the harbour of St Peter Port. It was
suspected they were taking troops from Guernsey to England to
help in its defence.

He had stood up and questioned the order, to his own
amazement, explaining that the trucks were probably carrying
tomatoes but he was ordered to sit down and was assured the
intelligence they had was accurate.

Over Alderney the *Gruppe* formed up into an attack formation.
One *Kette* of three aircraft left on a special mission to attack
"military" targets on the west coast of the island. Bernhard, at

the head of the remainder of the formation, headed south towards Guernsey which was glinting ahead of him in the afternoon sunlight.

The Bridge, St Sampsons, Guernsey

Lily had had finished work a bit early so she could do some shopping. She popped home for a wash and then went to meet Ma and the children at her house. From there they walked to the Bridge to visit the shops and get some food in for the weekend. They were sitting on their usual bench by the harbour at just after 6pm when they heard an unusual droning noise which seemed to overwhelm all of the other harbour sounds. People all around them stopped and searched for the origin of the sound.

Suddenly from the north, above the hill on which the ancient Vale Castle stood, several dark shapes flew towards them. The shapes were Heinkel Bombers from Kampfgeschwader 55 out of Villacoublay. There were 6 planes flying in groups of three and as they watched they changed formation and approached in line astern.

The group flew over the watchers on the Bridge and headed towards St Peter Port harbour.

Everyone had seen the black crosses on the wings and Lily was full of foreboding for her husband.

She turned to Ma.

'Ma, you head home. I'll take the children back to our house. I want to be home for when Laurie gets back.'

'OK love,' Ma replied seeing the concern in her eyes. 'He'll be alright,' she added to try and reassure her.

They hugged and went their separate ways.

Magloch House, Scotland

The weather wasn't as nice as it had been and it looked like it might rain. The girls spent the early morning helping in the stables as usual and then Mary made the decision not to go out in the carriage as they may get wet.

As they were stuck indoors Mary introduced the girls to the cleaners, Catherine and Sophie, who were to show them how to keep their room tidy and their bathroom spotless.

That meant they spent most of the day on their hands and knees scrubbing the bathroom floor or dusting, brushing, wiping and polishing every nook and cranny the cleaners could find.

The women seemed to take great pleasure in pointing out anything that had been missed and went around wiping their fingers along skirting boards and the tops of the doors until not a speck of dust was to be found.

The girls were told that every Friday this would be their job and they were expected to keep their rooms as tidy as the cleaners kept the rest of the house.

Finally, at around 4pm, Mary rescued them from Catherine and Sophie and ushered them down into the kitchen so they could help Cook prepare tea.

They were exhausted.

Rachel thought of her Mum and realised for the first time how hard she must work to keep their house tidy.

The three children were always making a mess but her Mum had never made her clean up after them, apart from maybe tidying away their toys.

That made her think of her family back on the Island and she hoped that everyone there was safe.

St Peter Port Harbour, Guernsey

The queue of tomato lorries at the harbour showed no sign of shortening. Each truck took its turn to pull up at the quayside and let the cranes do their work.

Laurence was on his third cup of tea of the afternoon and was looking forward to going home but the paperwork seemed never ending.

He was working overtime as the island struggled to ship all of the tomatoes that were being picked.

The postman had just made a special delivery. Dropping a bundle of letters on to his desk. Each lorry driver also left a delivery note. The pile on his desk never seemed to go down. Each note had to be checked and collated before the Isle of Sark, the last ship of the day, could sail.

The total weight of freight on the ship was a crucial factor as there were limits to the amount of freight each ship could carry.

The Isle of Sark was one of three ships on the Guernsey run and carried passengers as well as freight. A few people were milling around waiting for the go ahead to get on board for their trip to England.

The ship was moored right in front of his office and from where he sat he could see the Captain on the bridge. Laurence could also see that there weren't that many people waiting for this trip.

The office was noisy with people coming and going. A typewriter clicked away in the corner as Agnes, the office secretary, typed receipts and letters.

Outside of his window the cranes lifted tomatoes and dropped them into the ship's hold. Men were also carrying sacks on to the ship via narrow gangplanks.

If Laurence hadn't been focused on the paperwork he would have noticed that one by one men and women were stopping and looking north as word spread that a formation of planes were on their way. Laurence was adding another delivery note to his manifest when his tea cup suddenly rattled on its saucer.

The sound of the explosion came next as the first bomb dropped on to the harbour jetty about 200 yards from where he sat. Laurence rushed to the window. He could see a column of smoke billowing up from the clock tower near the bottom of St Julian's Avenue at the start of the pier. Columns of water were also climbing out of the sea in several places.

German planes droned overhead and as he stood at the window the glass in front of him shattered with the blast of another bomb as it landed on the pier. Laurence grabbed at his face and felt a trickle of blood running down his cheek. More explosions followed and Laurence rushed to the doorway.

From there he could see the skies above the harbour and the bombers attacking, lining up for their bombing runs. Explosions followed at regular intervals as each plane dropped their bombs.

Suddenly the sound of a heavy machine gun cut in to add to the noise of the explosions, as a team of gunners on the Isle of Sark started to fire back at the Heinkel 111s overhead. The noise was deafening.

More columns of water climbed into the air as several bombs missed the narrow jetty. Those that hit their target threw piles of debris into the air. He could hear the screams of people caught in the devastation.

People were running past his office and many were covered in blood. As the planes sped off into the distance, the machine gun stopped firing and all that was left was the sound of burning and screaming. It seemed like hours but within two minutes of the end of the raid he heard bells as the ambulances and fire engines rushed down St Julian's Avenue to the harbour.

But the planes weren't finished.

They swept around and coming in from the sea, opened up with their machine guns. The newly arrived ambulance was hit as it left with its first casualties and out at sea the Guernsey lifeboat was also machine gunned by one of the planes and a crewman was killed.

While this was happening, Laurence ran out of the office slamming the door shut behind him. Without a thought, he ran towards the smoke and fire. As he ran down the pier machine gun bullets seemed to follow him, making holes in the pier surface as they rushed past him. He ducked and fell, luckily, they missed. He got up and rushed into the devastation.

His army training and his service in Ireland prepared him a little for what he found. Bodies lay everywhere and the whole scene was made worse by the tons of tomatoes that had been blasted all over the pier. The area was a mass of red; blood and tomatoes mixing to create a horrific scene as if straight from the fires of hell. The smell was awful.

At the land end of the pier, the weighbridge clock tower building was alight, with flames pouring out of the roof. Tomato trucks he had passed in the bus on his way to work lay burning in a row. At least two had the drivers still in them, burnt corpses, slumped over the steering wheels. Other drivers had been cut down as they ran from their trucks and lay where they fell.

Laurence heard a cry and walking through the smoke found a young boy, badly injured, but alive. He had been in one of the trucks with his father and Laurence recognised the lad. His name was Jack Roberts.

He had also spotted the lads father, Frank, who was lying dead a few yards away from his son.

Laurence put his jacket under the boy's head to try and make him comfortable until the ambulance arrived. As he held the youngsters hand, the boy opened his eyes and smiled at Laurence. Laurence looked at the spreading pool of blood oozing from underneath the boy and knew there was nothing he could do.

He smiled back at the boy, 'Hold on son, the ambulance is on its way.'

The boy winced and in his pain thought Laurence was his father. 'Thanks Dad, where's Mum?' Tears were welling up in his eyes.

Laurence understood, 'She'll be here soon son, she'll be here soon.'

The boy smiled again, closed his eyes, took a last deep breath and died. Laurence held him in his arms and tears filled his eyes. His mind was full of images of his own children. He thought of the boy's mother, now a widow, having to bury her husband and her son. Hearing the roar of another plane he picked up the boy's lifeless body and oblivious to the danger, held it up the skies and shouted at the fast approaching plane.

'You Bastards!', he yelled. 'He was just a boy, HE WAS JUST A BOY!'

The Heinkel flew low over his head and he turned and watched it pass over him. More machine gun fire from the harbour flew past the plane but as quick as it came, the plane was gone, disappearing into the pillars of smoke, racing away from the devastated harbour.

People were now tending the injured and a policeman came up to Laurence to ask if he was alright. He could see the boy was gone and in the heat of the moment Laurence had forgotten his own small injuries. Blood was still running down his face from the cut on his cheek and he had several other smaller cuts on his forehead and also a cut on one ear from the flying glass.

He told the policeman he was fine and left the boy, now wrapped in his jacket to the ambulance team.

He stood and looked around him. Smoke rose high into the air from the line of burning trucks. There was also damage to the pier at the entrance to the Careening Hard and smoke was rising from damage to the buildings on the Cambridge Pier behind him, where fires were still raging.

A couple of small boats in the inner harbour looked a little worse for wear but there didn't seem to be any sunken vessels in the main harbour. The Isle of Sark was undamaged.

The air crackled with burning chip baskets and the smell of burnt tomatoes hit the back of his throat. The roof of the weighbridge clock tower had gone and the clock itself was stopped and badly damaged. Some of the timbers were still burning. He couldn't believe what had happened to such a peaceful place.

As he looked back towards town, windows everywhere had been blown out. Some of the buildings reminded him of skulls with dark voids where their eyes had been.

He walked back to his office and back to his desk. Glass was everywhere and barely a piece of glass was left in any of the windows. Amazingly one of the cranes was working already but in the office Agnes was hiding behind one of the desks. She looked up as he walked over to her, shocked at the sight of the blood on Laurence's face and hands. Before she could say a word, his phone rang. He answered it automatically, it was Lily.

How the call had got through he didn't know. Telegraph poles were pointing in all different directions as he looked back towards the devastation with cables hanging as low as the floor in places.

'Thank God!' she exclaimed at the sound of his voice. 'Are you alright?'

'I'm fine,' he replied, 'but a lot of people aren't.' He went on to explain what he had happened and what he had seen.

'Come home Darling.'

'I'll be there as soon as I can,' he replied.

The Aftermath

Around half an hour later Laurence left the office, he walked past the site of the bombing. Amazingly many of the bodies and some of the devastation had already been cleared away. One area was surrounded by ropes. A hand-written sign announced that there was an unexploded bomb there and to keep clear. Although the jetty was being washed down by the fire engines, there were still tomatoes lying in the gutter and a few stains where oil and blood had mixed to leave their mark on the tarmac.

There was a line of burnt-out vehicles which were yet to be moved, some still stacked high with burnt chip baskets.

Tarpaulins covered the cabs of the several of the trucks, their drivers were still to be removed.

Men were already working on the roof of the weighbridge clock tower using fire engine ladders, ensuring the fire was out and the roof was secure. Against the grey granite pier wall a single bunch of flowers had been laid. More would no doubt follow as news of the raid spread around the island like wildfire.

At the windowless newsagents in the Pollet, one of the main shopping streets in St Peter Port leading to the harbour, a banner announced many dead and wounded in the raid. No communication from Germany had been received as to why this crime had been committed.

The island's head, the Bailiff of Guernsey, had sent a protest to Germany according to the special edition of the paper that had already been printed. It also stated that he had sent a message to England telling the UK Government of the attack and requesting assurances that the information, that Guernsey was undefended, had been made known to Germany.

In the Air above St Peter Port

Bernhard had lined up his Aircraft on the Model Yacht pond to the south of St Peter Port harbour and approached over Salerie Corner. As he got nearer to the harbour he watched Willie lining up the bomb sight on the queue of lorries and he could see the unmistakable red of the tomatoes through the gaps in the chip baskets on each lorry.

He asked Willie how long before he could release the bombs and asked for a count down. When Willie got to five he pulled the bomb release and was rewarded when his bombs landed short of the main pier.

He noticed gunfire from one of the small ships and one of the K's started to fire back. He tilted the Heinkel away from the port and then circled to see what damage was being done. As he approached the harbour over Castle Cornet, he could see burning tomato trucks as many of the other Heinkels were successful with their runs.

The clock tower at the entrance to the harbour was alight and people were running everywhere.

To try and see more, so he could finally confirm the huge mistake they had made, he came in low over the devastation and then once again the anti-aircraft fire from the small ship in the port came his way.

Down on the pier he could see a man holding up what looked like a child's body.

He could not believe what they had done.

As they sped over the harbour he felt the plane shudder and he knew the plane had been hit. He swung the Heinkel to his right and headed out to sea in the direction of France. Tears filled his eyes at the sight of the dead child. He knew this was war but that was murder, he hadn't signed up to attack defenceless people.

He turned to speak to Willie and noticed he was staring straight ahead and looked very pale.

He touched him on the shoulder.

'Are you all right?' He had to shout over the engine noise.

Bernhard could see Willie mouth a reply but could not hear what he said. Bernhard leaned across and turned Willie's face to his and then realised something was badly wrong. Tears were streaming down Willie's face.

Bernhard called Kai, one of his gunners up to help Willie and as the gunner came to his side he spotted the blood pouring down the side of Willie's seat.

'He's been hit!' he shouted. Holding up his gloved hand which was now covered in Willie's blood.

'Call Kass up here to help.' he ordered and undid his harness and Willie's. He got Kass to clamber over him to take the controls and showed him how to keep the plane steady and where to go.

He then helped Kai drag Willie back into the plane and tried to stem the blood using a field dressing they had in their first aid kit.

Kai was shaking his head. The bullet had hit Willie near his right hip and gone up though his body, it was probably lodged in his lung. He was drowning in what was left of his blood while much more was draining away. Bernhard had now put a dressing on the damaged hip but despite the gunner putting pressure on the wound they could do nothing for Willie.

Bernhard checked that Kass had the plane stable and sat with his friend. He ordered Kai back to the guns to keep watch for enemy planes.

He knelt over Willie and held his hand. He felt some weak pressure and knew he was still alive. He bent over him as he could see Willie mouthing some words.

'Get the boys home safe Bernie'. He choked on the words. 'Tell my parents I love them.'

He coughed, and blood seeped from the corner of his mouth.

'I will Willie,' Bernhard whispered in Willie's ear.

There was a hint of a smile on Willie's face and then his grip on Bernhard's hand released. Bernhard was distraught and tears streamed down his face but he knew he had a job to do and he clambered back to take the pilot's seat.

He took over from the frightened gunner and powered the aircraft back towards France. 30 minutes later Bernhard landed the aircraft safely at Villacoublay. This time there was no round of applause.

Bernhard was struggling with what they had done and the loss of his good friend. He now knew he had been right about the tomato trucks and needed to make sure everyone knew the mistake they had made. He was convinced the island was undefended and could not believe that bombers from their Staffel had been ordered to attack.

He was determined to voice his views at the debriefing.

St Peter Port, Guernsey

Laurence spent some time talking to people he knew as he waited for his bus. Names were starting to be mentioned, names of the people who had died. He knew several from his years of working on the harbour. The father and son lived not far from him in the parish of St Sampsons.

Frank Roberts and Laurence had often spoken to each other at Church on special occasions and Jack had been in the same class at school as Rachel. Jack was his only son, they had even discussed their decision to keep Jack in Guernsey.

The most telling information he picked up was from an Isle of Sark crew member. He heard that her Captain had delayed the sailing to enable more passengers to join the ship as this was likely to be the last boat to leave Guernsey.

Despite the warmth of the weather Laurence shivered, he went to pull his jacket tighter around him but remembered where he had left it. He was going home in just his shirt and tie. He was also going home with a new determination.

On the bus home rumour was rife that the British were sending troops to the island and that the navy would be sending a ship to defend the harbour. Others were more pragmatic and hoped that the lack of response from the island would convince the Germans that they were not worth attacking again. It was also suggested that the remaining population would be evacuated but he knew that wouldn't happen.

Once again as the bus made its way north, German planes appeared on the horizon. One of a pair of Messerschmitt 109 fighters peeled off and flew low over the harbour. The pilot was probably surprised by the lack of visible damage.

However, closer inspection of the reconnaissance photos would reveal the tarpaulin over the burnt-out roof of the weighbridge clock tower building, the burnt-out trucks and a row of craters now filled with gravel where bombs had hit the tarmac on the pier.

The planes formed up again and flew east towards the Cherbourg peninsula, disappearing into distant clouds that seemed to be gathering over war torn, and now occupied, France.

Peace returned to the island and Laurence got off the bus at the Halfway and once again walked home. He noticed black ribbons were already hanging from the windows of Frank Robert's house.

Villacoublay, Paris, France

Bernhard stood in front of the Oberstleutnant of Kampfgeschwader 55. The argument in debriefing had ended in a fight and it wasn't looking good for Bernhard. He had got into a serious argument with the Oberleutnant holding the debriefing, and when he was told that the raid was in the best interests of Germany and Hitler, he had lost what little composure he had left and in a fit of rage, attacked his superior and had to be dragged away by the rest of his crew.

Striking a senior officer was not recommended in the Luftwaffe.

He was severely reprimanded and then told he would be stripped of his new rank. The Oberstleutnant then told him he would be transferred back to HQ and dealt with formally there.

As he turned to leave the Oberstleutnant called him back.

'Bernhard, I know you were right and I know you are upset at losing your friend but we must do as we are told, you and me both. This is the Luftwaffe and we must obey orders.'

He then did a strange thing, he saluted Bernhard, not the Nazi salute as favoured by Oberleutnant Holstein, but a regular salute and offered him his hand. Bernhard shook his hand and the Oberstleutnant wished him 'Good Luck'.

'You are a good man Bernhard. I will be adding that to my report. I hope they treat you well at HQ.'

Bernhard was stunned. He muttered a 'thank you Sir', and left the Oberstleutnant's office. He had two letters to write.

When he got back to his billet he started his letter home to explain to his parents what he had done. He guessed it would never reach them. He began to wonder if he would ever see them again.

He stopped writing and began his hardest task. It was the letter to Willie's parents. A long time ago he had been alone with Willie's father at a party when they got their first posting.

He sat remembering the day and how he had promised that proud man with tears in his eyes that he would look after Willie and bring him home. Now Willie would be going home in a coffin and Bernhard had been unable to keep his promise.

Sleep was a long time coming that night.

Guernsey, Friday Evening

Lily and Laurence hugged just that little bit longer than usual. She didn't even notice that his jacket was missing.

'I was so worried about you darling', she whispered in his ear out of earshot of the children.

She produced a handkerchief and licking it, stroked dried blood away from the cut on his cheek.

She already knew about Frank Roberts and his son as she had been to see Frank's wife to offer her support and condolences.

'Dadda, Dadda!!' Michael cried out rushing into his father's arms, there was no sign of Laura. 'Laura's in her room,' Lily told him, noticing the look on his face.

She explained how the news about Jack had reached her and she was so upset she had gone to her room in tears.

Laurence held Michael close and together with Lily they walked through to the parlour and sat down on the sofa. Laurence sat next to his wife with Michael on his lap. Michael knew things weren't right but was too young to understand grief and what it meant. They chatted for a while about the sights and sounds of the day and then Lily got up to make a pot of tea. Michael was soon bored and ran off to annoy his sister.

It was amazing how important a cup of tea was to the family. A cuppa seemed to be at the centre of all discussions and had a way of making things right.

Before she could put the kettle on Laurence called her back.

'Lily we need to talk. You have to go to England – now!'

Lily sat there in a state of shock. 'Now?'

'Yes dear, now. They are making final preparations for the Isle of Sark to leave and I think she'll be the last boat to leave Guernsey before the Germans arrive. We can't waste any time, finish packing your bag now and I'll take you down to the harbour.'

He followed her as they went upstairs to finish packing, she was in a complete daze. She had never left the island before and apart from the possibility of finding Rachel had no wish to leave her home and Ma.

'Where will we go?' she asked.

'That's a good question.' Laurence replied. 'What's left of my family live in London which is certainly not a good place to go. My brother is serving on HMS Hood and you can't stay at his anyway as they'll have no room in their small house for you.'

'Maybe they'll give us some accommodation in England,' Lily suggested.

'We can but hope, that will be down to you.' Laurence replied.

'Don't you think we should stay? The Germans probably won't come here, why should they? This is such a small place.'

She seemed to be trying to convince herself.

'I know my love but we are British soil and they may like the idea of capturing the islands before they go on to invade England.'

'If they do that we might as well stay here.' Lily replied.

Lily paused for a moment. 'Anyway, what did you mean that would be up to me?'

They were interrupted just then as Laura came in, followed by Michael, looking for some supper.

Lily smiled at her, she looked drained from crying. 'What's happening Mummy?'

Lily, seeming to make up her mind, ushered Laura back to her room and explained they were going to find Rachel. That seemed to cheer her up. Lily got her a small bag and asked her to pack some things for her and Michael, she left Michael with Laura and then came back to her husband.

She could see the tears in his eyes.

'I can't come with you dear, they won't let me on the boat. I'm too old.'

'I can't stand the thought of being away from you Laurie, we've always been together. The only time we haven't spent the night together was when the children were born. It would be unbearable Laurie, unbearable.' Lily started to cry and Laurie wrapped his arms around her.

They kissed long and hard.

'We won't be apart for long my darling. Whatever happens I will find a way to be with you.'

'Promise.' Lily pleaded.

'I promise Darling,' he said looking her straight in the eye.

Packing continued in earnest as she grabbed a few essentials and packed them into a small brown travelling case that had been her fathers, in itself a treasured possession. But what else to take. Her eyes scanned the room and she saw her wedding photograph and a family portrait that had been taken one happy Saturday afternoon in town.

Quickly she took them out of their frames and packed them tight into the lid of the case. On a whim, she ran into Rachel's room and spotted a ragged looking knitted rabbit her mother had made for Rachel when she was a baby. That too was squashed into the small case.

Lily took the picture of her father from the mantelpiece and put that with the other photographs. The room suddenly looked empty but she felt her father was with her, giving her strength for what lay ahead.

They rushed out of the house just in time to catch a bus going into St Peter Port. They sat in silence for most of the journey, holding hands with the children on their knees. By the time they got to town, the cordon at the end of the pier was being manned by several policemen.

Laurence explained that he was a member of staff from the Southern Railway. He was ushered through and walked with Lily towards the ship that would be taking them away from him.

She was amazed at the damage to the Weighbridge Clocktower and how bleak the pier looked in the fading light. Damaged vehicles were still dotted around the pier and she could see that a part of the wall along the edge of the quay was missing.

It seemed life had suddenly become very different. The ship's horn sounded, a mournful sound that left everyone silent for a moment as the echo bounced around the small town of St Peter Port. Conversation, cries, yells and tears soon recommenced and they stopped next to the policemen who were checking people's credentials.

'I don't think I can do this on my own,' Lily whispered to Laurence as they stood looking at the waiting boat.

'You can do anything my dear.' Laurence said, trying to reassure you. 'I'll be with you soon. Just get the children to safety and everything will be all right.'

Laurence produced the three tickets and after one last hug the policeman waved them through and they were gone.

Lily walked down the jetty to the waiting boat, tears streaming down her face, her small case in one hand and with her other hand she held on to Laura, who in turn was holding Michael's hand.

Every few steps she looked back but couldn't see Laurence through her tear-filled eyes. Together, hand in hand the three of them joined the short queue to get on the boat.

Laurence stood alone for a moment, he had never felt so lonely in his life. Once he saw them finally get on the deck he backed away from the throng and headed away from the quayside. He asked a passing crewman what time they were sailing.

'In an hour or so mate' was the gruff reply.

He turned and headed home.

On the Boat

It was chaos on the boat, people were milling around everywhere and Lily sat on a bare bit of deck with her back to a cabin wall.

She sat in the evening sun, Michael and Laura sitting on either side, their two small bags either side of them and tags on their coats which had been given to them as they boarded.

She was crying quietly, ignoring the sight of the Victoria Tower glowing in the sun. The little ones seemed excited that they were going to find Rachel. Lily had told them that they would see their father soon so there wasn't any concern on their part that he wasn't going with them.

So much was happening there was little time to take it all in. None of them had ever been on a boat before. Hundreds of people were milling around, many were trying to find somewhere to sit and soon all of the space along the cabin walls had gone. Others were lining the rails trying to get a glimpse of people on the shore. Most people had been prevented from getting on the jetty so only a few police, harbour workers and government officials were there to see the boat off.

'Where's Dadda?' Michael asked for the umpteenth time.

'He's coming.' Lily lied. 'We'll see him soon.'

'Why are you crying Mum?' Laura asked.

'Just happy to be having a trip on this boat, Laura love,' she lied again. 'Can't wait to see Rachel too.'

They had been sitting watching the sun set over St Peter Port for over an hour and it was now almost dark when the boat finally sounded its horn and a plume of black smoke swung away into the sky from one of the two funnels. They all jumped out of their skins with the shock of the deafening sound.

A large white flag with a red cross flapped from the forward mast. A few people cheered and some were waving to people on the shore who were waving back. Most of the adults had tears in their eyes, they were leaving home and had no idea when they would be back.

Ropes were cast off and the deck started to shudder as the engines started to turn the giant propeller under the stern of the boat.

Slowly the bow swung out and the boat headed into the centre of the harbour before swinging towards the open sea. Rows of fishing boats pulled at their ropes and a few small sailing boats made a vain attempt to follow the steamer. People on the small boats waved frantically, obviously family of people on board.

Lily imagined Laurence looking out to sea from their home at the Halfway and watching the boat sail past.

When would she see him again? What would happen to him if the Germans did occupy the island?

The Captain sounded the ship's horn three more times in a sad farewell to the island. The mournful sound echoed around the harbour.

This would probably be his last trip to Guernsey for a while and who knows where the war would take him after this.

As he steered the ship towards the harbour mouth, staff at the lighthouse at the end of the breakwater gathered together to wave at the ship as she left. People from Castle Cornet also came down to the breakwater and waved furiously at the ship as it passed by.

They knew, as did everyone else that this would probably be the last ship to leave the island before the Germans arrived. Passengers lining the ships rails waved back and took in every detail of the island as they left. They too wondered when they would see their home again.

Lily didn't wave; she just held her children and wept quietly. Her heart was back on the island, no thoughts of home, her mother, the rest of their family and friends entered her head. It was her husband she thought of, and the injustice and cruelty of having to leave him there and make her way to England on her own with the children. He had promised he would see her again soon but she couldn't imagine how that could happen. Another tear rolled down her cheeks from her red swollen eyes.

They passed the lighthouses each side of the harbour mouth and headed out into open water. The skipper ordered full ahead and the ship leapt forward. Most people had moved to the other side of the ship to see Guernsey disappear astern. Lily stayed where she was. It had gone cooler in the shade so she pulled the children in tighter to keep them warm.

Herm slipped past as they headed north towards England and the unknown.

Into the unknown

The boat was now at full speed heading north. The islands were firmly behind them and Alderney lay ahead and beyond that a new life for the hundreds of souls on board.

People had come back to sit where there was space and every corner of the deck was full, with people sitting in family groups. Some played cards, others read books but most simply chatted about what lay ahead.

Michael was asleep on Lily's lap and Laura was singing nursery rhymes to herself. Lily had stopped crying, she had run out of tears. A few people had recognised her and said hello but she preferred to keep herself to herself. Her husband, best friend and soul mate wasn't with her and there was no-one else she wanted to speak to.

A hand on her shoulder made her jump and woke her from her thoughts and she was instantly annoyed at the interruption. She didn't look up as she didn't want to talk to anyone, nor did she want anyone to see her tear stained face.

Then she felt a kiss on top of her head and her heart skipped a beat. She looked at the hand and the gold wedding ring which sat on such a small finger gave the game away. She looked up and her heart almost stopped. Laurence smiled down at her.

'I'm here love.'

It was the understatement of all understatements. He knelt not to disturb Michael and she flung a free arm around his neck.

'Oh darling. I love you.'

She found more tears, but this time they were tears of joy.

He picked up a beaming Laura and settled down next to his wife.

With Laura on his lap they immediately snuggled in together. Lily was exhausted but happy at last.

She looked at him more closely and realised he was wearing what looked like a sailor's outfit.

'Lost another jacket Love?' she laughed.

'This time it was in a worthy cause my Darling, not a sad one.'

He smiled at her and put his arm around her shoulders.

For a while they were quiet. They had left everything behind them. Laurence only had the clothes he stood up in. They had very little money between them and one change of clothes for the children. Laurence had the house key in one pocket and what little savings they had in the other. Everything else they possessed was locked in their home.

As if by magic he produced four apples and shared them around.

Lily smiled, *he is so considerate*, she thought. Eventually she asked him how he had got on board and he told her the story.

After they had said their goodbyes he had left the harbour and ran all of the way home.

Laurence had quickly made the decision to try and get on board and had changed into a white vest and dark blue trousers, just like the sailors he had seen on the docks. He had put on his black jacket and a cap and got his push bike out from the back yard. Having pushed the bike through the house and robbed the biscuit barrel of their savings, he found a paper and pen and wrote a quick note to Ma.

Dear Ma

I am so sorry. I decided today after the bombing that Lilian and the children needed to go to England to be safe.

I am going to try and go with them but if I don't get on the boat I will see you tomorrow.

This war can't last forever so if we do all get away I am sure we will be back by Christmas and having our usual celebrations.

I will write and tell you where we are.

Keep safe.

Laurence xx

He didn't bother putting the note in an envelope. Ma had a spare key to the house so he knew she would find the note later today or tomorrow.

He took one last look at their lovely home. He checked upstairs, tidying some toys on Laura's bed and put Michael's football on his pillow. He went to Rachel's room and looked at the dinner jacket on the bed. He straightened the bow tie he had placed above the jacket as if it was around his neck and smiled as he thought of the last time Lily had straightened his tie.

He checked the kitchen and found a bowl of apples. He tucked two is his trouser pocket and dropped another two down his shirt. He looked around the front parlour, which seemed bare without the photographs, before checking the back door was locked. Satisfied that all was neat and tidy he locked the front door and rode off as fast as he could towards the harbour.

Laurence knew the pier was fenced off from public access and that he wouldn't be able to get down to the jetty so as soon as he reached the Royal Hotel he rode down the slipway, opposite the hotel, on to the beach. He leant his precious bike against the sea wall and walked towards the sea.

Thankfully the tide was quite low and he could reach a set of steps which were built into the pier wall. Sneaking up the steps he peaked over the wall and noticed a policeman on duty at the top of the steps.

The policeman was busy watching the small crowd queuing to get on the Isle of Sark and in the evening light didn't notice Laurence sneak behind him and head off towards toilets at the end of the jetty.

Once inside he took off his jacket and his cap and tucked them down the back of one of the toilets. Wetting his hair in the sink he combed it flat and put his comb back in his pocket.

He walked out of the toilets and headed towards the dwindling stack of sacks full of post and other cargo waiting to be carried into the ships hold.

As he walked, he watched the small group of sailors carrying the sacks into the ships hold. Each picking up a sack, putting it on their shoulder and then walking down the plank on to the ship.

They made it look very simple.

Once on the ship some dropped their sacks on the deck but others carried the sacks down a ladder into the hold.

He timed his walk until the last of the group of sailors was on the plank and confidently picked up a sack, hoisted it on to his shoulder, and followed the sailor gingerly down the gangplank and on to the ship.

Halfway along the plank he made the mistake of looking down and nearly lost his balance. He could see the water between the ship and the jetty sloshing about and for a moment lost his confidence and had to pause for a second before completing the short walk on to the ship.

A ladder led down into the hold and, keeping his head down, he carefully climbed down into the darkness.

'Hurry up mate,' one of the sailors shouted at him, but he ignored the comment and walked to the back of the hold.

It was almost pitch black in there.

He placed his sack on top of some others and, with a quick look around, slid down into a gap between the sacks and the metal wall of the hold.

He held his breath as more sacks were stacked around his hiding place and a net full of goods was dropped in to last gap in the hold by one of the dockside cranes. As the ropes attached to the net were undone, the sailors climbed back out and he heard someone shout.

'That's the lot skipper.'

Next thing he knew the hold cover was being fastened down and he was in locked in. He heard the engines start and felt the vibration of the screw and then the motion of the ship before he clambered out from his hideaway. He could just reach the top of the hold by clambering on the sacks and when he was sure the boat was out of the harbour he had started knocking on the hold cover. Eventually one of the crew let him out.

Two of the sailors marched him up to Captain Golding but after hearing his story and finding out he worked for Southern Railways he had let him go to find his family.

And now here they were, all together again.

Lily had sat quietly while he explained how he had sneaked on board and at key moments she had squeezed his arm which was still wrapped tightly around her shoulder. She kissed him again and broke the intense silence that followed the end of his story.

'Well my darling, now we are all together life is good again. We don't know how long we are going to be away but we must live for each day. Let's enjoy this new adventure and try to find Rachel. We both know how to work hard and we can make anything work as long as we have each other.'

Laurence smiled. 'That was just about the longest speech you have ever made.' He hugged her closer yet.

'And every word made perfect sense.'

Epilogue

Saturday the 29th June

Apart from a distant sighting of a group of aircraft and the frantic scrambling of the ship's gun crew, the trip to Southampton on the English south coast was uneventful.

The children slept for some of the journey, lulled by the gentle motion of the ship. They had passed two British Warships as they neared the English coast and for the first time in a traumatic week, Lily felt safe. They docked in the pitch black in Southampton harbour, the lights out policy was in full force against the potential night time air raids.

Men with red torches led them from the ship on to a waiting train. The family found themselves in a small cabin with a single mother and her daughter. Michael sat on his Dad's lap and fell back to sleep and eventually the train set off on the long journey north. They had no idea where they were going. The train travelled through the night and stopped several times on the journey.

Dawn found them in at a station in the Midlands. After being given some time to stretch their legs and get a welcome cup of tea they were off again even further north.

The Guernsey papers reported that 22 people had died in the raid and another 35 had been injured. 6 planes had been seen but there could have been more and a few of the dead were identified. A Policeman, a popular crew member on the lifeboat, which had been strafed while at sea, and an Ambulance driver who had been tending to the injured.

Five people had also been killed in Jersey.

Damage around the harbour was extensive, the buildings on the Cambridge Berth had almost been destroyed, telegraph poles had been left in disarray with wires hanging everywhere. The clock tower of the Weighbridge was heavily damaged and there were large holes all down the quay. Windows in buildings all over the area of town near the harbour had been blown out.

The island was in a state of shock. In total around 17,000 people had left Guernsey, almost half of the population.

It seemed everyone left waited with bated breath for what would come next.

Sunday the 30th June

In Guernsey, on the 30th June 1940, a single German aircraft landed at Guernsey Airport, the pilot had a quick look around and was met by a local policeman. An official from the local government met him and the island formally surrendered to him. He returned to his aircraft and flew back to France.

Later in the day three Junkers JU-52 aircraft landed in Guernsey. Troops quickly left the aircraft and fanned out across the airport. There was no-one there to oppose them or welcome them. They took the Union Jack down from the airport flag pole and replaced it with a swastika.

Monday the 1st July

Rachel's letter dropped through the letter box of her empty home.

The local papers ran a front page setting out the Orders of the Commandant of the German Forces in Occupation of the island of Guernsey.

They were quite simple:

1. Curfew would be from 11pm to 6am.
2. No trouble should be caused for fear of serious consequences including the bombing of St Peter Port.
3. All orders must be obeyed.
4. There would be no provision of alcohol, all stocks to be locked up.
5. No entry to the Airport is permitted.
6. All weapons and ammunition to be handed in by 1pm today.
7. All servicemen on leave in the island to report to the Royal Hotel
8. All boats to stay in port
9. The sale of petrol is suspended, except for essential vehicles, permits will be issued to essential vehicles. Private use of vehicles is forbidden.
10. The blackout should continue to operate as it did before the occupation.
11. Banks and shops are to open as normal

Signed on the 1st July 1940.

And so, the occupation of Guernsey began.

October 1945

The journey home did not take place until over 5 years later. In October 1945, five months after the Germans on Guernsey surrendered to British troops, Laurence and Lily began their journey home. The journey almost felt as strange as the one they had made in the dark over 5 years earlier and the weather was awful. They had received just a few short, heavily censored, letters from Lily's mother and did not know what they would find. Michael remembered nothing of Guernsey and Laura precious little. Rachel wondered if she would meet some of her friends again and what their little house would be like.

At least this time they had a few more belongings with them and in his pocket Laurence carried their precious house key.

When they arrived, they found German bunkers, a railway line and tons of abandoned equipment everywhere. A rudimentary bus service was running and the family caught the bus to the Halfway and walked the short walk to their house. On the way, they joked about whether Laurence's dinner jacket would still be lying on Rachel's bed when they got home.

The bus had been virtually empty and they saw very few people walking along the front. No-one spoke to them as they made their way home.

Laurence put the key in the lock and the door swung open before he could turn the key. The lock had been forced.

The house was empty, not a thing was left, even the carpets had been pulled off the floor. Lily and the girls just burst into tears and Laurence walked from room to room, making sure that at least the house was secure.

It would take them until Christmas 1945 before the house was back in some form of order, mainly with the help of Lily's mum. Lily always suspected who had been responsible for stealing their furniture but common sense prevailed and nothing was ever said, after all it had been awful under occupation and luxuries like new furniture had not been available. Lily never spoke to one neighbour ever again, as she believed she had taken her precious settee.

They also had rationing and a lack of work to contend with. Laurence having got used to manual work in the north of England, found a job working on the completion of the new reservoir, which had been started before the war. Lily was soon working in greenhouses growing tomatoes and life slowly returned to normal. Rationing finally ended in 1954. That same year Lily's first Grandchild was born to Rachel and the war became a memory, best forgotten.

Lily and Laurence never left their island home again.

As for Bernhard, the report of his fight was somehow lost and he continued flying sorties over the UK, some said they needed the pilots and couldn't afford to lose one as good as Lucky Bernhard.

As the pressure on London increased he was increasingly, but not exclusively, taking part in raids over London. On one raid on Bournemouth during November of 1940, which should have been an easier mission than the Blitz on London, his plane was damaged. He tried to get to Guernsey airport but eventually crashed on a group of rocks called Crevichon, between the islands of Herm and Guernsey.

He was killed along with all of his crew.

His dream of visiting Guernsey again came true in a way as the bodies of the crew of the Heinkel were buried in the German Military Cemetery in Fort George on the outskirts of St Peter Port.

Guernsey still lives with the physical relics of what is now part of History. German bunkers, anti-tank sea walls and the Underground Hospital are the most obvious "mementos" of those terrible times.

Laurence and Lily are sadly gone and only their children carry memories of that life changing time. So, we can never ask them, just how hard it was to make such a life changing decision, to evacuate a home, venture into the unknown and leave your family, friends and possessions, during 10 Days, one Guernsey summer.

Rachel's Story

Rachel had a wonderful time in Scotland but when she was eventually sent back to her parents in 1942, to join an English school in Bolton, it was to a strange existence. She really didn't want to leave Scotland. The beautiful house she had lived in with all of her friends had been a paradise for her, compared to the terraced house in Guernsey, and all she could picture of Bolton was factories, bombing raids and grime.

Eventually the family were all reunited and she would grow to love Bolton and carry fond memories of the town for the rest of her life. She would form at least one lifelong friendship with a girl she met in Bolton and revisited the town several times. She also developed a strong Lancashire accent which took years to disappear, and which Lily hated.

When she got back to Guernsey she excelled at school but in her late teens developed tuberculosis and was confined to bed for almost a year. She recovered and went on to work in a variety of jobs before marrying one of the island's top football stars. He too had been evacuated but he had spent much the war in the Taunton area.

They both had their own businesses and enjoyed a comfortable and fruitful life. They are still living in the island. They brought up two children of their own.

Michael and Laura's Story

Michael went back to school when he returned to Guernsey and developed a love of carpentry, inspired by his father. He went on to be happily married in the island and had three boys. His wooden creations still win prizes to this day.

Laura was a figment of my imagination for the purposes of this story but will always be close to my heart.

Laurence and Lily's Story

Laurence and Lily ended up in Bolton where they headed up a house with several more Guernsey children. While Lily ran the house, Laurence got a job in a munitions factory and before long, life had settled into a new routine, brightened by the occasional letter from Rachel.

When they returned home, they worked hard to get their house back to the loving home it was before the war and restore some sense of normality.

When Ma became too old to look after her house they sold their house and moved in with her and lived there for many years. Lily worked in the greenhouses until she retired and Laurence went back to working in offices and spent many of his remaining years working for Huelin Renouf, a local freight company. He would cycle there and back every day and never did learn to drive. They all moved to a new bungalow in the 60's and Ma went with them, living well into her 90's.

One of my favourite memories of her was the way she would say hello to the Newsreader when he said hello at the start of the programme.

TV must have seemed like magic to someone born in the 1870's. How I wish I had spent more time with her and captured some of her memories.

Laurence played in the band into his late 60's but eventually succumbed to dementia and in time could only remember a few of us. I visited him with Lily the day before he died.

Every weekend when Laurence was out playing I would spend my Saturday evenings and Sundays with Lily. We loved to play lotto with wooden counters and watch the Billy Cotton Band show and Morecambe and Wise.

She also loved watching snooker on TV and seemed to worship Hurricane Higgins, for some reason.

Lily too lived into her mid 90's, never stopping work until she had a stroke while Rachel was on holiday. I climbed through the window to get to her as she had locked herself in the house the night before. My sister had called me as she was worried as Lily wouldn't answer the door. She lived on for the best part of year in hospital. I visited her nearly every day and it was her that told me much of this story.

They say you can pick your friends but you can't pick your family. Well I for one could not have picked a finer family, nor a finer upbringing.

There is no doubt Guernsey is a wonderful place for children to grow up, and in the 50's and 60's, as the island recovered from the occupation, every day was an adventure.

The Family

From left to right:

Michael, Lily, Laurence, me, Rachel (with cat) and Ma circa 1958

Glossary:

Blitzkrieg - Lightning War! An intense and fast moving military campaign designed to bring about a quick victory. The main German General associated with the term was Heinz Guederian who recognised that the use of tanks, with wireless communications, could lead to swift success in warfare.

Kampfgeschwader 55 – Battle Wing 55
Aufklarungsgruppe – Reconnaisance Group
Gruppe – Autonomous unit of the Luftwaffe
Staffel – Squadron
Kette – Sub Unit of three Aircraft, literally a chain.

Ranks of the Luftwaffe
General der Flieger – Air Marshall*
Generalmajor - Equivalent of Air Commodore
Oberstleutnant – Wing Commander
Oberleutnant – Flying Officer
Major - Equivalent of a Squadron Leader
Feldwebel - Equivalent to a Staff Sergeant
Unteroffizier - Equivalent to a Corporal

*Hugo Sperrle at this point of the war was a General der Flieger. Within weeks of the occupation of the Channel Islands he was promoted to the rank of Generalfeldmarschall (Marshall of the Airforce) and was given his Ceremonial Baton of Office by Hitler himself.

Guernsey Gache – This is a traditional Guernsey Fruit Loaf, absolutely delicious as long as it has lashings of Guernsey Butter on every slice!

A La Perchoine – Guernsey French for Until Next time or until we meet again.

Acknowledgements:

With thanks to Kai Junghanns for his research into the German involvement in the bombing of St Peter Port. Also to Ryan Cirigliano for his proof reading skills.

Thanks also to the Priaulx Library for letting me carry out my research through their archives and providing such excellent support.

I have also carried out research through the Internet and Wikipedia has been an invaluable resource as well as Youtube videos of the Heinkel 111.

Heinkel He 111 by Karl-Heinz Regnat provided some excellent information about this particular aircraft.

Hitler's Wartime Picture Magazine - Signal, edited by S L Mayrer was also a useful reference book. Interestingly it references that the Magazine was printed in English and sold in the Channel Islands during the years 1940 – 1944. I have never managed to find one of those magazines.

Finally, the Channel Island Transport Fleet Histories, Volume I, Bailiwick of Guernsey, published by W J Carman, gave me valuable information about the buses that ran during June 1940.

The names of all the main characters in this story have been changed but some names of historical interest are correct. The timings of the events have been adjusted slightly but events recorded on each day are by and large correct as reported in the media of the time.

About the Author

Tony Brassell

I started writing Ten Days One Guernsey Summer some time ago and now 77 years after those traumatic days it is finally finished. In many senses, it has been a labour of love as time to write hasn't always been easy to find.

I was born and raised in Guernsey and have lived here all of my life. I spent a lengthy career in the Civil Service, acquiring a wide knowledge of Guernsey and have a keen interest in the island's heritage and culture, in a wide range of areas.

For many years, I was known as the island's native guide, within the Civil Service, and have escorted VIP's at the highest level, including a Deputy Prime Minister, when they have visited Guernsey.

When I left the Civil Service, I established a local tour company called Experience Guernsey Limited and operated that business until 2008. I am now working as a Business Advisor with the Guernsey Enterprise Agency, trading as Startup Guernsey (www.startup.gg), helping people to get started in business. I am also the Branch Office for the IoD Guernsey Branch.

As well as the day jobs, I build, host and maintain websites for businesses and private individuals through the domain www.bestplace4u.co.uk and in what little spare time I have left I love to write.

My unique perspective on Guernsey, through a lifetime based on the island, and having family that have lived through this terrible period in the island's history, inspired me to write this story.

Please remember it is based on historical fact but is a work of fiction. The names of the main characters and identifying details have been changed to protect the privacy of individuals and some elements added to give balance and perspective to the story. Any resemblance of the main characters to actual persons other than my family, living or dead is purely coincidental.

Throughout the whole book there is one inescapable fact. At one point my Grandmother took her children and left my Grandfather to get on to a boat not knowing when she would see him again or where they were going.

He wasn't prepared to accept that they would have to live apart and risked everything to keep them together. In that respect, I feel this is primarily a love story.

It was love that drove every decision and in the end, it was love that kept them together.

I hope you enjoyed this book, my first but hopefully not my last, novel.

A La Perchoine (Until next time)

For more information with pictures of some of the key locations mentioned in this book, visit:

www.10daysoneguernseysummer.com

Printed in Great Britain
by Amazon